CHAPEL COVE ROMANCES

WHEN LIFE BEGINS AT FORTY...

A Chapel Cove Romance
~ Book 2 ~

By

ALEXA VERDE

Cover by Marion Ueckermann. Contact Information: marion.ueckermann@gmail.com

Edited by Deidre Lockhart.

Cover Image ID 128056506 purchased from Depositphotos © oneinchpunch
Logo Image Chapel ID 164957864 purchased from Depositphotos © verity.cz

ISBN: 9781093863604

This book is dedicated to Andrea Byers.

Andrea, thank you so much for all your support you're giving Christian authors, for your friendship, and your kindness!

PROLOGUE

Friday, April 12

"OKAY, I'm ready to make my list of things I want to do before forty!" Laughing, Kristina Vela snatched a piece of paper. Hmmm, at barely thirteen, she'd take *forever* to reach forty. But if her friends decided to make such a list at Reese's slumber party, she was game. "First and foremost, I want to serve the Lord, follow the path God is giving me."

"I like that," Naomi said quietly as she perched her glasses up on her nose. Her voice was often quiet and her demeanor, as well. No wonder, with a horrible mother like hers.

Not Kristina. She spoke her mind. Sometimes she was too outspoken.

She chewed on the tip of Reese's black pen, a habit she'd tried to get rid of.

Then the pen slipped from her hand and bounced on the thick carpet near crumbs of the cake they'd just finished.

Kristina picked it up. Though the carpet looked clean, that should help her not gnaw on the pen. "Second, I'll marry the love of my life and have a boy and a girl. Though considering that many of my relatives had twins—"

"Maybe you'll break that tradition." Reese chuckled. "And give birth to triplets!"

Kristina sent a pillow her way.

"Wowzers." Naomi's eyes grew big. "By the way, that's cramming two wishes into one."

"I'm just starting." Kristina giggled. This was fun. She wrote fast. "Third, I'll live in a large—no, *humongous*—white brick home with arched windows and a tree house in the yard. Nothing like our falling-apart house. My brother does his best to fix it however he can, but a boy can only do so much." She perked up. "It'll have roses in front. The color of the sunrise. The place will be full of laughter and sunlight and will always smell like fajitas or tacos or pastel de tres leches."

"You already thought a lot about it, didn't you?" Naomi crowded closer, compassion in her voice. What her friend lacked in confidence, she made up for in kindness.

"When you live in a reality like mine, you have to create a fantasy to hold on to." Kristina sighed. She'd had to grow up fast.

"Sorry," Naomi whispered.

"Anyway, fourth. I want… I want…" Kristina nibbled on the pen again. Oh, oops. She'd nearly tasted the carpet. Then she brightened. "Yes! To go to college and open my own business. I'd love to make other people's homes beautiful, and Roman already taught me how to handle a hammer and a saw."

Reese snorted. "Can you even *lift* a saw?"

They doubted her? Huh.

Probably because she was the smallest of them, even the shortest in her class. Kristina jumped to her feet and placed her hands on her hips. "A little one, okay? Just because I'm petite and poor, doesn't mean I can't strive for my dreams. I just have to work harder for it."

"We believe you can do it." Naomi rose and squeezed her in a tight hug, her hair tickling Kristina's forehead.

"Thanks." Gratitude warmed her heart.

After letting Kristina go, Naomi shot Reese a glance. "It actually sounds more reasonable than somebody else's dream here. A famous supermodel. Hmmm."

Reese, who at least had to outgrow her teenage zits and braces to become a supermodel, flipped her long strawberry-blonde hair back. "And I fully intend to achieve it."

"I'll pray for you. If that's God's will, it'll happen." As Kristina plunked back on Reese's bed, the bedspread embroidered with silver flowers fluffing around her, she grabbed the piece of paper and studied her list as if looking at it could make it come true. What else? "Mom always says she has to wait on tables and fall off her feet every night because she never got a degree."

Kristina's heart squeezed painfully. "And because Dad never makes enough to provide for us. I'm so tired of their bickering and shouting. My family will be nothing like that."

"You only have one item left on the list." Reese nudged Naomi. "Wait, she'll probably cram three things into that one."

"Why only three? Let me think." Kristina pursed her lips, then scribbled furiously. "Travel outside of Chapel Cove. I love my hometown, but I want to see other places, too. Maybe India."

Reese shifted on her bed. "She couldn't have settled for nearby Portland."

After shooting her a glance, Kristina continued writing. "Help my mom open a Mexican restaurant. Roman and I could fix up an old building. She loves cooking but says she never has time for it. Her fajitas and carne cuisada are to die for. Maybe then my mother will finally be happy, the scandals will end, and Dad will stop drinking. Oh, and help my twin brother achieve his dreams, too."

"I told you." Reese laughed. "That's three things?"

Kristina hiked her chin. "You know I love Roman. I can't leave him out of my list. Nooo!" She shook her head, sending her dark shoulder-length hair flying around her face. "Sometimes we can read each other's thoughts."

Naomi's face pinked. "I don't think I want to know what a teenage boy thinks."

"And he protects me from school bullies. Why don't people get that it's not my fault I'm the shortest in class and poor?" Kristina swallowed hard as she gestured to the worn-out clothes everybody knew were bought at a thrift store.

"We'd protect you." This time Reese pulled Kristina into a hug.

"But it's good you don't have to." Her mind whirling, Kristina hugged her friend back and raised her shoulder in defense as she eased back. Think. What else? "Oh, and one more thing. I should do something crazy. Parasail. Bungee jump. Snowboard from a mountain. Something."

"And that's coming from a person who only wanted to list five things." Naomi gave her a playful swat.

"Yeah." Kristina stared into space. She'd seen too much in too little time and learned things she'd never wanted to know. But things would change when she graduated high school. She couldn't wait to grow up. "I just realized something, girls. We should never limit our dreams to only five things. I believe God has many, many more wonderful things for us."

CHAPTER ONE

Twenty-seven years later…

A WEEK to freedom or to the biggest disaster of her life?

Kristina Langley, soon to become Kristina Vela again, sat up in her bed and hugged her middle.

She rocked back and forth in the tiny wooden-frame house she was renting back in her hometown, Chapel Cove. It smelled of dust beyond its white walls, white ceilings, and white tile floors. Morning sunlight filtered through white curtains onto white furniture. Talk about a blank slate.

As much as it screamed for color, she could do nothing in a house that wasn't her own. Just like Cullen hadn't let her do much in their mansion.

He won't be my husband for long. Only a week until my marriage of twenty-two years will be over.

She'd left Portland the day after her dear Cullen filed for divorce and kicked her out of the house and his life. His promise to send her things had never materialized. Thankfully, she'd had enough clothes and toiletries packed for her previous trip to Chapel Cove, and she didn't need much.

First, she'd stayed in her childhood home.

Kristina swallowed hard as she hugged herself tighter. Her mom, unhappy that the monthly checks would stop now, wasn't shy about expressing it.

One bright part about this was having the opportunity to help her brother, Roman, recover after a motorcycle accident.

The lump grew bigger in her throat. She needed to think about a life of her own. Her divorce should be final in a week. Her stomach churned over seeing Cullen again.

"Only one more time." She climbed out of bed and dragged herself to the bathroom.

Tile chilled her bare feet, but she didn't look for slippers. Her heart felt colder than the tile. Colder than ice.

Ice.

Ice cream.

No, chocolate cake. That would make her feel better. And she could take it to Roman for breakfast.

Yes! She brushed her teeth furiously, welcoming the refreshing minty flavor. So what if it wasn't a healthy breakfast? One couldn't go wrong with chocolate, and with her divorce—the symbol of her marriage failure and her broken heart—so close, she was entitled to some sweetness, wasn't she?

Chocolate also helped her think, and she really needed to figure out what she was going to do with the rest of her life. She was turning forty in a few days.

Forty!

Wowzers. She nearly shuddered as she wiped her face with a towel, the fabric soft against her skin, the lavender laundry-soapy smell doing nothing to improve her mood.

Anyway, that was her excuse to get the delicious chocolate cake, and she was going to stick with it.

She lifted her head and lowered the towel, and in the mirror, sad brown eyes blinked back at her. A few tiny wrinkles lurked there somewhere. Her hair hung thin and mousy. And yes, she had a gray hair or two. She cringed as she plucked out a few.

Ouch. Ouch!

No, she needed to stop this.

Okay, so she showed her age. So what? Like she was going to look for romance now! She brushed her dark hair, barely below her chin, and sprinkled an expensive flowery perfume on her wrists, one of the reminders of her previous life.

Some people said life started at forty.

Huh.

She snorted as she pulled on her baggy blue jeans and comfy black—to match her mood—sweater. No need or wish to dress up anymore. Those people didn't have to start their life back in their hometown, without a degree, husband, or work experience. One good thing, her daughters had already turned twenty and were in college. With all Cullen's faults, he'd keep paying for their degrees.

Lord, please help Leanna and Reanna not to suffer because of our divorce. In Jesus' name, amen.

After grabbing a coat and grinding her teeth, she left the house and braced against chilly Oregon March air and occasional drizzle. But the air wasn't nearly as chilly as Cullen's gray eyes for the past decade.

I'll find my path again.

And right now, that path led to chocolate.

Soon she was on the way to Aileen's Pastries, her old sedan growling, as if unhappy to be woken up. She had to buy this car because, sure enough, Cullen had decided to keep her luxury car. But then, she didn't expect anything less from him.

Her mouth watered over Aileen's incredible cake with melted chocolate inside and outside, plus almonds, pecans, and a secret ingredient Aileen wasn't disclosing.

Oh yes.

Aileen made only one cake of that kind a day, so getting to the pastry shop early enough to snatch it was important. With Kristina's weakness for chocolate, she'd learned it soon enough.

A sapphire-colored truck was already parked near Aileen's Pastries. Huh. She'd better hurry. She had a chocolate cake with her name on it.

The bell rang as she rushed inside. Warm air carried delicious scents of the colorful assortment of cookies, cakes, and pies.

Hmmm. Empty beige walls could use some décor. Maybe have a brighter color and hang large pictures or even paintings with cupcakes, pies, and Christmas cookies. And add colorful peach tablecloths and fresh flowers in fun vases…

Stop daydreaming.

She'd often imagined how she could change the interiors of the places she'd visited, but when she'd told Cullen some of her ideas, even about their place, he'd laughed. Claiming she had no taste, he hired an interior designer to do everything in the house according to his, which meant she had to live among charcoal-gray colors and strange metallic furniture.

Then she stopped.

A tall, well-built man with dark hair, dressed in an aquamarine sweater and black slacks, stood near the counter. She'd never seen him in Chapel Cove, but then, she'd been living in Portland for twenty-two years.

And... And... He was pointing at *her* cake!

Nooooo! She wasn't about to wait another day to taste such deliciousness.

Kristina married to Cullen would hightail out. But she wasn't going to be that Kristina any longer. Over two decades of being a doormat were more than enough.

Squaring her shoulders, she marched to the counter. "There are so many great cakes and pies here. Just look at that peach cobbler. Are you sure you want the chocolate cake?"

Aileen looked from Kristina to the man and back, an unsure smile on a pretty face covered in freckles like her cupcakes were covered in sprinkles. Thankfully, no other customers had entered.

"Positive." His tone clipped, he scarcely spared her a glance.

Well, well, well. If not for his rudeness, he could be rather handsome—if she cared for thirtysomething men with broad shoulders, athletic physique, impressive muscles, smoldering blue eyes, and chiseled features. Which she didn't. Her mouth watered purely because of the chocolate.

Purely.

She foisted off a smile. "I'd really like to have that cake, please."

Aileen's smile strained at the edges. Her freckles, now pronounced, wobbled above it. "I'll have a new cake in the afternoon."

Hmm. An improvement from a day's wait, but Kristina could already taste gooey deliciousness.

And it didn't matter if she acted like a child. She'd given up so many things during her marriage—her self-esteem, her chance at a career, probably even her dignity. She wouldn't give up this.

She grabbed the cake box. "Then this gentleman can have one in the afternoon."

"Ma'am." At last, he turned to her. "With all due respect, I'd like to have this one."

Startled by the pain in his eyes, she let the box slip from her hands and land on the floor. Kristina gasped.

A muscle moved in his strong chin. Then he shook his head, pivoted, and left.

"I'll pay for it." Stifling a twinge of guilt, she handed Aileen cash.

The woman, whom Kristina knew well in high school, mostly because Roman had dated her before things went wrong, sighed. "He told me his little daughter begged for a chocolate cake this morning. I heard through the grapevine, he's moving to Chapel Cove from Portland. His wife died two years ago. Such a tragedy."

And Kristina had taken a candy—ahem, *cake*—from the kid.

Swallowing a bitter taste, Kristina sank near the box. She hadn't cried when Cullen had mistreated her or when she'd fallen and bruised herself and still had to make his dinner. Or when she'd found out about his infidelities—the ones that apparently never stopped.

But now a lonely tear slid down her cheek. She'd worked so hard not to be like her mom, to avoid arguing and trying to get her way. She'd done her best to have a large home and a loving family, unlike her childhood.

And she'd lost it. Besides everything she'd worked so much for, she was losing herself and didn't know how to find her way back. After being silent and submissive, did she have to go the opposite direction and deprive a poor child and her father of a small joy?

Lord, please forgive me. Please help me fix this.

After Cullen kicking her out like old shoes, she wasn't sure God answered her prayers anymore, but she had to keep trying. She'd prayed so hard for her marriage, but it collapsed, anyway. Her faith, once so strong, wavered in the past years.

Forgive me, Lord.

She handed Aileen more cash after discarding the ruined cake. "Please find out his address and send the chocolate cake in the afternoon with my apology. And… Hold on. Give me half a dozen of those chocolate cupcakes."

As soon as Kristina got them, she sprinted out of the store. Hopefully, she wasn't too late.

Yes! She nearly did a fist pump. The man was talking to his daughter in the booster seat in the back of his truck cab. A loud wail nearly deafened her. Okay, maybe rather *trying* to talk because she doubted any words could pass that sound.

Kristina's heart nearly broke all over again, and she slowed her steps. She didn't want to face an angry father and a crying daughter, especially if she'd caused those tears and anger.

She straightened her spine. For years, she'd done her best to avoid conflicts when Cullen had blamed her for everything, any mistake their daughters made, a tiny speck on the dinner table, or an extra ounce gained. It wasn't her fault she was petite and any extra ounces were noticeable.

Lord, what should I do?

She felt a slight nudge in the back. Okay, she had to face this and try to remedy the situation. Her step faltered, but she forced herself to approach the truck.

"Um, I'm so sorry for what happened." She nearly had to yell. "As a way of apology, I brought these cupcakes."

Maybe they didn't compare to the cake. But chocolate was chocolate, right?

The man sent her a glare, but his blue eyes softened when the wailing stopped. "Chelsea, look at what we've got here. Mmmm, they look soooo good. Do you want to try one?" He stepped out of the way, probably to provide a better view of cupcakes.

Kristina smiled at an adorable child with an upturned nose and curly sandy-blonde hair framing a round tear-streaked face.

A chubby hand reached out. "Yeah!"

Wishing the truck was a bit lower or she was higher, Kristina made two attempts before she managed to climb into the back seat. Good thing she wasn't wearing a skirt, or it would've been embarrassing, especially balancing the cupcake box. Inside smelled like cherry air freshener.

Unless the girl's father would lift her... An inexplicable wave of heat rose up her neck. Thankfully, with her dark skin, it wouldn't be too noticeable.

She opened the box. "Um, maybe I should help you with this."

Too late. Uh-oh.

The girl grabbed a cupcake, and soon the dark, gooey mass smeared her face, hands, cute pink jacket with carnation-colored flowers, and tiny blue jeans. Some of it somehow even ended up on Kristina's sweater.

"Yummy!" The girl gave her stamp of approval as she reached for another.

Kristina sent the guy an apologetic glance. "Sorry about the mess."

He shook his head. "I'm glad you had the idea to bring those cupcakes." His voice lowered. "Her mother used to bake the world's best chocolate cake."

She couldn't even imagine Leanna and Reanna growing up with Cullen and without her, and compassion squeezed her heart. Poor child. It couldn't be easy for the kid's father, either. "Aileen's Pastries has a few tables and a restroom. How about you enjoy some of these cupcakes with a cup of coffee while I help your daughter clean up?"

Wow, those bright eyes matched his aquamarine sweater. Her heart skipped a beat. That couldn't be a spark of attraction, could it? She wasn't divorced yet, and even then, if she never started dating after Cullen's insults, it would be too soon.

She simply remembered how difficult raising the twins on her own was, with Cullen always absent at work or never-ending dinners with his friends. She wanted to help this grieving single father. Yes, this was the reason.

The man's eyebrows rose. "You'd do that for a stranger?"

For the first time in years, she chuckled. "You're in Chapel Cove. You'll find out soon there are no strangers here. People know each other and help each other. Besides, I should make up for that ruined cake."

His brows narrowed, shadowing his eyes. "Thank you, but that's okay." He probably figured letting his child go with a person he'd just met wasn't safe.

She removed her wallet and driver's license and showed him her ID. "I'm Kristina Langley. My maiden name is Vela. And I really am who I say I am." Okay, maybe that sounded strange. She put her ID back into the wallet. "You can ask Aileen if I'm trustworthy. Or… somebody else you know in town. Many of us know each other here."

An inner struggle reflected on his handsome face. "I don't know people in Chapel Cove yet. Well, besides my former in-laws."

Then he glanced at his daughter and fished his cell phone from the slacks' back pocket. He seemed to send a text to someone. The reply beeped nearly immediately. He read it, nodded, slid his phone back, and hesitated for a few more seconds.

Kristina's heart made a strange movement in her chest.

A light smile touched his lips as he leaned to his daughter. "Chelsea, would you like some tea or juice? And let's get you cleaned up a bit."

"I don't wanna clean up." The girl's petulant voice rose a fraction.

Uh-oh.

Think fast.

Kristina pulled out a small plastic elephant from her purse. She'd carried it with her ever since little Leanna had given her toy to her as a present. "See this elephant? His name is Taco." Okay, that was a weird name, but that was what Leanna had called him. Maybe because her girl adored the fish tacos Kristina always made from scratch. "He wants to drink and have a bath. How about going to the restroom here and giving him a bath?"

Big baby blues blinked at her. Eyelashes still carrying tear droplets fluttered. "Okay. Come here, Taco. I gonna give you a bath."

Swallowing that bittersweet taste again, Kristina handed the child the iris-colored toy, the symbol of her daughter's love, so close to her heart. Once upon a time, Leanna had looked up at her with the same trusting expression. Once upon a time. Now, Leanna refused to talk to her. Cullen obviously brainwashed his daughters, especially Leanna, who with black hair and gray eyes was like him in appearance and character.

Kristina's heart constricted. But it was what it was.

As she stepped from the truck, her foot caught in some toy. Argh!

Her arms shot out, and she tried to hold onto something to avoid meeting asphalt face-first. How embarrassing!

Strong hands caught her. For a brief moment, he held her and then eased her to the ground. He smelled of expensive cologne and the ocean, and she had difficulty finding her voice as a warm wave rippled through her.

Stupid, stupid, stupid.

I've given up on men forever.

And I need to remember that.

CHAPTER TWO

GREG MATTHEWS said grace before taking a sip of strong, black, flavorful coffee. A lump formed in his throat. He had difficulty praying after Sally's death, but since marrying her, he'd never skipped saying grace before a meal.

Was he reckless letting his daughter go to the restroom with a stranger? Of course, he was. Even if his former in-laws had met her before and the pastry shop owner seemed to know her well.

What a fool he was!

He plunked the cup on the table so fast the liquid sloshed over and jumped to his feet.

Worry fisted over his heart. What was he thinking? He did his best to be a good parent, but he kept making mistakes. Maybe unforgivable mistakes.

"She'll be back soon." Aileen, while attending a customer, threw the words to him.

As if to prove her statement, two pairs of footfalls sounded along the tile. And... giggles. He stared at his precious child holding Kristina's hand with her tiny right fingers and clutching the toy elephant in her left. A skip in his girl's step jostled her pigtails, and a smile bunched up on her now-clean face.

Chelsea's laughter rang sweet music to his heart. She hadn't laughed since... since Sally was gone.

The fist loosening its grip, his heart shifted in his chest.

Thank You, Lord.

"Daddy! I gave Taco a bath." She let Mrs. Langley's hand go and ran up to him.

He scooped her up, and warm gratitude sluiced through his veins as he held his daughter close again, safe and sound. His life revolved around Chelsea now, and so it should.

"I appreciate it, Mrs. Langley," he whispered in the direction of the woman he'd hated minutes ago for stealing his daughter's chocolate cake.

"Please call me Kristina." Large, doe-like brown eyes gleamed. "I was happy to help."

He shook her hand. "Call me Greg, please. And this is my daughter, Chelsea."

The girl wriggled in her direction. "Wanna eat cupcakes with us?"

An uncertainty in her eyes, Kristina raised her chin at him. "I don't want to intrude."

"You won't. I'd love for you to join us." His chest warmed as he pulled out a chair for her. He meant it. He was curious about this petite woman with dark hair and sad brown eyes.

Seeing the ring gleaming on her ring finger and remembering Langley was her married name, he swallowed a strange disappointment. It really shouldn't matter whether she was available or not. Either way, he wouldn't be interested.

"Would you like a cup of coffee? Or anything else?" He placed Chelsea on a chair.

"A cup of coffee would be great. But I'll get it." The lady walked toward the counter.

"Daddy, Taco said he wants a muffin. Blueberry." Chelsea put the toy on the table.

"Elephants don't eat muffins." He suspected Chelsea and that toy would be inseparable. "And you had enough sweets for today."

Her lower lip stuck out. "Daddy, we can't leave Taco hungry."

His heart turned to mush. He'd traveled dangerous slopes and opened several stores, but he was such a pushover for his daughter. "Okay, just sit here quietly. I'll get Taco a muffin." That sounded strange even to his own ears.

At the counter, he whirled around to keep his daughter in view.

"She's so precious." Kristina smiled at him.

Something soft and sincere about her smile touched him. "I hate that she has to grow up without her mother." Pain sliced him inside.

"I'm so sorry for your loss." Her eyes darkened.

Oh, well. They said it was easier to talk to a stranger.

As the line shifted, he watched his daughter and lowered his voice. "If I could've died instead of Sally, I would've. I'd give all my blood, drop by drop, to keep her alive." Once he started talking, the words tumbled out. "She was amazing. I knew she was the one for me the moment I saw her. It took me two months to persuade her of the same and another two months to talk her into marrying me. I, well, dated a lot before I met her and had a certain kind of reputation. And her parents didn't like it that I was into snowboarding and risked my life on high slopes."

Without saying a word, she listened, leaning close, her flowery perfume as subtle and pleasant as the woman herself.

"I moved from Colorado to Portland for her, and we opened a sports equipment business. When she said she fell in love with me, I couldn't be happier. And then I realized I was wrong when Chelsea was born. I became so incredibly happy. But now, when Sally is gone..." He couldn't push more words past the lump in his throat.

His daughter, a spitting image of her mother, pushed the purple elephant along the table, muttering something.

"It must've been very difficult for you and Chelsea."

Why would he say all these things to this woman when he couldn't tell them to anyone before? After condolences and a few awkward visits, most friends and relatives had scattered away, as if not knowing how to help.

Only two more customers remained in front of Kristina, so he hurried to speak before he returned to Chelsea. He couldn't let his daughter overhear anything sad. "Sally taught me so many things. She taught me to pray, to see beauty in every day, to cook things Chelsea likes to eat, even to bake a marionberry pie. But one thing Sally never taught me." His throat constricted again.

"How to live without her." Kristina's whisper was barely audible.

Still, he heard her clearly because those words were imprinted forever on his heart.

Only one customer left. His precious kid sipped on her juice and waved.

"When Sally was dying in the hospital, tears escaped her eyes. I thought she was hurting, asked her whether I needed to call a nurse. She said it wasn't about being in pain or even dying. She was going to be with Jesus soon. But she was aching that it would be difficult for Chelsea and me when she'd leave us behind. That was the kind of person Sally was."

And then she'd told him that one day he'd meet a new love and a new mom for their daughter. That woman would be like a ray of sunshine, beautiful, warm, and soft, and still, he'd fight his attraction to her nearly as much as Sally fought hers to him.

The image conjured up some tall blonde the way Sally was, so petite brunette Kristina couldn't be it. And he'd never allow himself to be attracted to a married woman. Well, this was his wife's fantasy to comfort him, anyway.

"What would you like?" Aileen's voice ripped him out of memory land.

Kristina didn't say anything, so he glanced at her. Two tears were trickling down her cheeks. The depth of her compassion reached inside him.

"Kristina?" Aileen's voice rose. "Are you okay?" She handed her a few tissues.

"Yes." Kristina took the tissues and dabbed at her eyes. "A cup of coffee. One creamer, no sugar."

"I'll pay for it." He hurried to add. After talking to her, he could breathe a little easier as if the tight band around his lungs let go a bit. "Are you sure you don't want anything else?" He gestured over scrumptious desserts.

"I'm sure. And thank you." She picked up the cup, and the wonderful aroma drifted to him.

He purchased a blueberry muffin and strode back to the table. He pulled out the chair for Kristina again, and she sat down.

"Daddy, Taco said he doesn't want the muffin anymore and I can have it," Chelsea announced.

Yes, that was to be expected. "Here we go, sweetheart."

A sting of guilt reminded him a good parent shouldn't be feeding his daughter this kind of food. He'd fed her healthy meals in Portland, always cooking them himself. Considering her severe shellfish allergy, getting takeout was risky. He really needed to either rent or buy a house in Chapel Cove where he could cook again.

Borrowing his former in-laws' kitchen grated on his nerves, even if they were the reason he'd moved to this little town. They wanted to spend more time with their granddaughter.

He claimed a chair near her.

"Thank You, Lord, for this muffin and for Miss Kristina and for Taco. Please bless our food. And please help Daddy so he starts smiling again, amen." She bit into the dessert.

Though he was grateful for his daughter's faith, he needed to teach her not to hide behind the elephant's back. How was he supposed to figure out these things by himself, without Sally? Asking Kristina to help wasn't an option. His gaze flicked to her wedding ring again.

"You shared your story, so it's only fair I should share mine." She sipped coffee from her elegant porcelain cup. "I'm separated and about to be divorced. I have two daughters, twins, in college. I grew up in Chapel Cove but lived in Portland after getting married right out of high school. And now my husband found a younger and more beautiful replacement." She glanced at the child, and her hand flew to her mouth. "I'm sorry. I probably said too much."

Thankfully, Chelsea seemed to be occupied with the muffin and Taco.

So Kristina was pretty much single. A wave of relief flushed over him. There was no reason to feel that way. No reason whatsoever.

Hating the misery in her eyes, he leaned forward. Her husband had to be an idiot to let a woman like her go. "Maybe younger but more beautiful? I doubt that."

"Oh, you're just being nice." She waved him off.

He took a sip of his own flavorful coffee and studied her features over the rim. She had the largest, most expressive eyes he'd ever seen, a delicate nose, and an attractive mouth, so he wasn't just being nice. But her confidence seemed to have taken a hit during her marriage.

"At least, help yourself to the cupcakes. You bought them." He pushed the box her way.

She plucked one from the box and bit into it. "Mmmm, this is delicious."

A speck of chocolate dolloped her lower lip, so it really wasn't his fault he looked at her mouth. "Um, you've got something right there."

"Oops." She wiped it with a napkin.

For an inexplicable reason, his heartbeat increased, and he needed to find a distraction—fast. "I'm moving to Chapel Cove and have no idea what I'm going to do here."

Great start. Now she'll think I'm an idiot.

To his surprise, she nodded. "Welcome to the club. I'm feeling the same. Though, since Chapel Cove is my hometown, I probably have it easier. You said you used to snowboard and have your own business, right?"

"Yes. I also worked as a ski instructor in Colorado. After I moved to Portland, we opened several sports equipment stores. They became rather successful. I sold them all before deciding to move here. I'm taking a couple of weeks off to spend more time with Chelsea…. And then… I guess I'll figure it out. What about you? What do you like doing? Where have you worked before?"

"I like fixing things. Imagining the way a house would look like inside, and—" She checked her watch, winced, and drained her coffee. "I have to go. I'm supposed to meet my brother in a few minutes." She waved to his daughter. "Bye, Chelsea. Bye, Taco."

The girl waved back. "Bye, Miss Kristina."

"Wait." He leaped to his feet. "Um, Chelsea and I would love to have your phone number." He looked for help to his child, and she nodded and lifted the toy. He scrambled for an excuse. "In case, you know, Taco would miss you." He cringed. This was lame. So lame. Now *he* was hiding behind a toy elephant's back.

A soft smile touched Kristina's lips. "It's a small town. I'm sure I'll see you, Chelsea, and Taco around."

As she walked to the exit, a strange feeling rippled through him as if he really hoped he'd see her again soon.

"Daddy, can we have a tree house here?" Little feet stomping against the grass, Chelsea ran to him.

Greg squatted and opened his arms for a tight embrace from his five-year-old. "Of course, honey." He inhaled the mango scent of her favorite shampoo as she leaned to him, so trusting, so fragile that his heart skipped a beat.

Knowing how life could be cut short, he sometimes had difficulty letting her go.

She wiggled out of his embrace. "And a puppy, right? He'll be happy here." She gestured her chubby hand to the large yard, plenty of space for a puppy to run.

"Well…" He stared into light-blue eyes, just like her mother's, and a lump formed in his throat.

Moving to Chapel Cove was difficult already, as was dealing with his in-laws. They'd lost their only daughter, as they'd shouted, because of him, and their granddaughter was all they had left. Getting a puppy wasn't on the agenda.

"Pretty-pretty please?" Her lower lip stuck out adorably.

His daughter had him wrapped around her little finger. And she knew it.

He patted her lovely curls, so soft under his palm. Just like her mother's. He pushed the thought away as the lump grew bigger.

Tears prickled behind his eyes, and he wasn't ashamed of them but couldn't let his little girl see them. "Let's get a place to live first."

That was a tall order, considering the town's housing market wasn't large, and the real estate agent—she'd said to call her Amy—had already shown them all the luxury homes. Chelsea had nixed each one. Amy had admitted she'd only brought them here because she'd run out of everything else.

Watching his step, he lifted his child over the broken porch to the patio door where white paint peeled off. The floor squeaked as he stepped inside, and the place smelled of wood and dust. The ceiling, a scary gray color, seemed to shroud the debris piled up in the living room.

Frankly, he didn't hold his breath for this place, either. Well, maybe he did have to hold his breath, but only because the smell wasn't great.

He placed Chelsea on the floor. "Don't run. I don't want you to trip over something." He snatched her hand.

"Miss Kristina can come visit us, right?" She coiled her whole hand around his index finger.

His heart made a strange movement in his chest. He'd been so angry with the stranger who'd ruined the chocolate cake his daughter wanted. But when the woman had shown up with the cupcakes, she'd been so nice. And last night, Chelsea went to sleep with the little elephant.

Framed by suntanned skin, Kristina's beautiful brown eyes seemed to look into his very soul. Petite, she'd appeared well proportioned, though he rather guessed the latter than could see under her baggy dark clothes. But judging by the way she was talking about her ex-husband, she clearly wasn't looking for romance.

Neither was he. Then why this sudden increase in his heartbeat?

He gestured to the debris. "I don't think we can bring Miss Kristina here yet."

"We'll fix it up." His girl tugged on his hand. "Let's go see my room."

His eyebrows shot up. "*Your* room?" He wasn't sure whether to smile or cringe.

"Yeah! Over there." She dragged him along a hall with walls so dark they were nearly black to a room off the right. A large arched window offered a windowsill that could easily support a child. "My bed will be over there. And puppy can sleep over here. And I want elephants on the wall. That way Taco won't feel lonely."

"Are you sure?" He looked around, trying to see the room through her eyes. "Maybe we should go look again at the other homes we saw. They are larger and… cleaner. Move-in ready." Not to mention, more kid-friendly. "And we could get some of those chocolate cupcakes on the way you liked very much."

Not a wise idea to bribe a child with chocolate, but if this wasn't desperation, then what was? His heart overflowed with love for his girl. "So, what do you say? Look at those homes?"

Chelsea tugged at his hand again and smiled. "Let's go back to the yard, Daddy. I'll show you where a swing's gonna be."

He'd die for that sweet smile. Something warmed inside him. Maybe coming to Chapel Cove could heal Chelsea's heart. As for his own, it would be broken forever. "A swing?"

She tilted her head to the left and sighed out exasperation as if he couldn't understand simple things. "Gotta have a swing!"

"Well, if we gotta, then we gotta," he muttered under his breath as his palm swallowed her tiny fingers and he followed her.

Hiding a grimace, he lifted her over broken boards on the porch. This house should come with a hazard warning, and he'd be crazy to buy it.

"Here. A swing's gonna be here." She pointed at a large maple tree.

While Chelsea ran around the yard as if already chasing the invisible puppy, he fished his phone from his jeans pocket and pulled up the internet. A few people did repairs and upgrades in town. Roman Vela had excellent reviews. His website showed before and after pictures. Impressive work.

Hmmm. Vela... Kristina's maiden name? Must be a coincidence. He pushed the beautiful image out of his mind.

A bird chirruped in the tree, and his girl giggled in delight. He scooped her up and placed her on his shoulders, so she could see the tiny chickadee better. "You know, two of the houses we saw had swimming pools inside. Wouldn't you like to swim in a pool?" He'd have to keep a close eye on her, but making her happy would be worth it.

Chelsea quieted. Aha. The thought obviously appealed to her. He took a full breath of air filled with the scents of grass and foliage as if he could nearly smell the victory.

Then she squealed. "Daddy, look! A squirrel! Yay!"

Yeah. So much for that. "Don't try to pet her. They bite. They have sharp teeth. And squirrels don't come with the house. They come and go as they please."

"I like it here." Her voice grew quieter.

The squirrel scampered in the branches and then over the fence, which, by the way, was missing a number of boards. Something else to fix before a puppy could move in.

Greg put his child on the ground and squatted to her eye level. "The house will need to pass an inspection. Electricity, plumbing, roof, all that. And even if it passes, it's going to be a lot of work to fix this house." It might be silly to talk to her like she was a grown-up, but sadly, his daughter had to grow up too fast.

"I can help you paint. You'll just need to lift me so I can reach far. Miss Kristina can help. She said she likes fixing things."

He nearly groaned. Miss Kristina again. As lovely as the woman was—after the cake incident cleared up—it wouldn't be wise for his daughter to get attached to a stranger. He needed to distract her fast. "What color would you like to paint your room?"

Pondering that important question, Chelsea tilted her head. "My room will be pink."

For the first time since his wife's death, he chuckled. "Will the elephants be pink, too?"

She shook her head, sending those adorable curls flying around her face. "Of course not!" She thought a moment. "They'll be purple. Like Taco."

His heart shifted in his chest. He wanted to give her everything he could, purple elephants and all, to help her reach as far as possible, but he couldn't compensate for what she'd lost.

He scooped her up again to avoid all the hazards on the way through the house to the driveway in front, where Amy was waiting in her car.

The mango scent of Chelsea's shampoo making his rib cage constrict, she leaned against him, and he could nearly hear her little heart beating. "Daddy, Taco told me he wants to visit Miss Kristina."

Well, what was he going to do? "Sweetheart, we don't even know where she lives."

"Grandma says it's a small town. Easy to find people."

Gently hugging Chelsea's tiny frame, he carried her through the house. The thought of seeing that woman again wasn't entirely unappealing. His pulse increased. Or maybe it was too appealing, and that wasn't good.

He'd never, ever be able to survive the second heartbreak. Everything inside him was still aching after Sally. "We'll see about that."

When he knocked on Amy's window, her bored expression hinted at her expectation of another lost sale.

His embrace tightened around his girl. "Are you going to tell Ms. Amy, or should I?"

"Oh, I gonna tell her! This is gonna be our home." A bright smile illuminated Chelsea's face.

And for that, he'd be cleaning debris and repairing the fence himself if needed.

Amy's jaw slackened. "Do you mean...?"

"Yes. Chelsea and I are going to buy this house."

CHAPTER THREE

A WEEK later, Kristina sank onto the soft cushion of the nearest chair in her rented home, and her fingers wrapped around the hard edges.

She became a divorcee. The word tasted strange, foreign, and slightly bitter.

The trip to Portland and back hadn't wiped her out as much as the meeting with her husband. True to his word, he'd tried to take everything, and he knew the best ways to do it. There was a reason he was one of the most successful divorce lawyers in Portland. At least, she knew he'd continue to pay for their daughters' education, apartments, and cars if she gave up on her share of their marital assets.

"You should've let me punch him." Crutches clicking against the tile, Roman walked from the door and sat down at another wooden chair he'd made himself.

Due to the bone healing wrong, the doctors in Portland had to rebreak it and put it together again to ensure it healed right, so he'd had to be on the crutches way longer than he'd hoped.

Roman's large, muscular frame, chiseled by years of physical labor, and sharply angled features made it difficult to tell they were twins. He'd towered over her since they'd been teenagers. But they did have the same brown eyes, dark hair, and a bond they'd shared since birth.

She traced a finger over the smooth surface of the oak table he'd also made. This wooden hand-carved furniture suited her better than the weird expensive metallic pieces she'd left behind. Those had felt cold and indifferent to her touch, just like their owner.

But seeing hatred on Cullen's face hurt so much. What did she do to deserve it? Her stomach tightened. Having Leanna take his side hurt even more.

Kristina wanted to curl up in a dark place and keep crying until she was completely spent. "Nah. If anybody should enjoy wiping that smirk from his face, it should be me."

"Finally! I recognize the old Kristina." Roman seemed to catch himself. "Not that you're old, *hermanita*. Um, would you like me to make you a cup of tea or something?"

Yeah, like she'd send her brother to wait on her on those crutches. Bad enough that his health care bills were piling up, and with him being self-employed, his income depended on his ability to do the job. He'd had to refuse too many clients already. She suppressed a grimace. But no, he'd never take a handout from her.

"Nearly forty and starting over." She resisted the urge to hide her face in her hands.

After Cullen's infidelities, she'd opened her own account and put some money there over the years, a fact that had nearly given him a heart attack. It was only ten thousand, a drop in the bucket compared to what he'd ended up with. But she'd give it all to Roman if he let her.

A drop in a *bucket...*

Her bucket list!

She searched her memory. Helping her brother was there. As well as getting her mother to open a restaurant.

Yes! She pulled her shoulders back. "Remember, when we were kids and I'd get upset over a lousy grade or kids teasing me, you'd say..."

He nodded. "If you want to feel better yourself, help someone else. That's what Dad used to say."

Leaning against the back of her oak chair, she figured it was best not to mention that their mother would always reply he should help himself first before doing free work for others. Maybe then, they wouldn't be so poor. "I went around the neighborhood and asked whether anybody needed to get any simple repairs done, free of charge."

"That was nice of you." Kindness softened his features.

"Useful, too. And better than wallowing in my misery. I did three paint jobs, one fence mending, and one assistance laying tile. I even helped with a plumbing project. I've got good referrals now. But maybe I could do a paint job for one of your clients. I'd like to help you with your repair business. It would be good for me to get more experience."

Roman's dark eyes lit up. "I'm glad you asked. I had a call today from Greg Matthews. He's a newcomer in town and just bought a house. It's structurally sound, and the plumbing· and wiring are good. Roof is fine, too. But the house needs a lot of work. Painting—walls and ceilings—and cleaning. Carpeting—but we can get somebody to come in and do the job. The fence needs mending and painting. He wants a tree house and a swing in the yard for his daughter. Obviously, I can't do the work like this...." Grimacing, he gestured at his crutches.

Bubbling with excitement, she jumped to her feet. "I'll help! I mean, I can't do complex work, but I'll clean and paint. And remember, we did the swing together when we were in high school? I'll let Mrs. Matthews decide on the paint colors, of course."

"There's no Mrs. Matthews, as to my knowledge."

"Oh."

Hold on.

Greg Matthews? It couldn't be the same Greg she'd met a week ago, could it? Her silly heart made a strange movement in her chest. Was it... Was it attraction? But "marrying the love of her life" once was more than enough. No more men. "Set up the meeting with him, and I'll go."

"Have I mentioned how much I love you, hermanita?" Roman grinned at her as he rose. "You're truly a treasure, and Cullen made the mistake of his life divorcing you. Now, let me take you out for a pizza. With extra-cheese, the way you like it. My treat."

Her dad had a point. Her stomach was still in knots, but some lightness inside her lifted the weight from her shoulders. "*Muchas gracias*. To celebrate my divorce?"

"Frankly, I'm glad your marriage is over. Cullen wasn't worthy of you. But I know it hurt you, so I wouldn't celebrate your divorce. I'd like to celebrate the beginning of your new life. New Kristina."

Her heart warmed. She was so thankful to God for giving her Roman. Even if she'd lost so many things, she still had something so precious. "I like that. New Kristina. No, the *real* Kristina."

The next day, silently praying for her brother, Kristina knocked on the only part of the reddish door where paint wasn't peeling. Glaring holes in the fence and squeaking once-white porch confirmed Roman's assessment. This house needed a lot of repairs and touch-ups. But so much the better for her brother and herself. More work meant more income for him, and she fully intended to share it with him, if not give him all of it.

This should be a good distraction from her failed marriage, too.

The door opened, and she stifled a groan.

Yes, it was that Greg. The man who made her heart beat faster. A man so attractive it was intimidating.

Great beginning of a new job.

Not!

Resisting the urge to flee, she plastered on a smile. Her brother needed this job, and she could keep her emotions in check. She had over twenty years of practice. "Good afternoon, Mr. Matthews. I'm here in regard to the repair work you requested from Roman Vela. I'd like to look at the house, and then if we agree to the terms we can start as soon as you'd like."

His blue eyes widened, their expression unreadable. He waved for her to enter. "No formalities needed. I told you to call me Greg, please. You're not Roman Vela."

Stepping inside, she nearly wrinkled her nose at the smell of debris and dust. "A smart observation." Oops! If only she could bite back her words. She had a sharp tongue as a teen, but she'd hidden it for two decades. Apparently, it came loose in the worst moment possible. "I mean, Roman is my brother. A twin brother."

How old was Greg? Early thirties? Definitely way younger than she was. With a black polo shirt hugging his well-shaped torso and muscular arms, he obviously worked out regularly. Even a five-o'clock shadow didn't ruin his image.

She'd never been the one to salivate over men.

Uh-oh. Hadn't she decided to give up on men for good?

This guy grieved his wife. Besides, most likely, he wouldn't consider dating a woman nearly a decade his senior, especially one he'd met under their circumstances.

His cologne smelled expensive. On a closer look, his clothes seemed expensive, too, and she knew the difference. Cullen would kill her if she'd bought him anything "beneath his status."

She turned her attention from Mr. Chiseled Features to the important matters, like the paint colors he wanted in different rooms or the kind of floors. She shouldn't be prejudiced against him if he was well off. Not all rich men were like her ex.

No matter.

No dating. Only work.

She needed to stop looking at Greg as if he were a prime rib steak and she was on a diet forever. Her mouth watered at the thought of steak.

Not helping!

"Please tell me the things you'd like to get done." She took out a notepad and a pen and started writing the list he was giving her.

Showing her the room his daughter had chosen for herself, he chuckled. "This one will need to be pink. With purple elephants painted on the wall, of course."

"Of course. How is Chelsea?" A longing in her heart surprised her. She couldn't get attached to that precious child in just a few hours, could she?

His face brightened. "She's with her grandparents for today. I wish she chose a different house so we could move in already, though. I don't like her living in a hotel."

His love and dedication to his daughter touched her. So unlike Cullen. And still, Leanna had taken his side.

Stop it!

No need to feel sorry for herself.

She threw back her shoulders. "We'll try to fix it as fast as we can." If she needed to work ten-hour days, she'd do it.

"By the way, Chelsea loves Taco." His lips tugged up. "Thank you for giving her that toy."

He had a very attractive smile. No thoughts like that!

"Taco?" Oh yes, the elephant. Maybe she could make them some tacos. She'd had to learn cooking early, and she made mean tacos. Even Cullen liked them.

No, no, no.

She pursed her lips to prevent words from escaping. Inviting this man and his child for a home-cooked meal would be a total disaster.

Total!

"It must be rough for her since..." Her hand flew to her mouth. Her future client's life and family were none of her business. No matter how much compassion squeezed her rib cage now.

"Yeah..." Shadow passed over his face. "And I have no clue what to do, how to make it better for her."

More compassion stirred inside her. "You'll find the way. I'll pray for you."

There was no better time than now. She said a silent prayer for his and Chelsea's healing. Praying for them was easier than praying for herself. Maybe because she knew exactly what to ask for while she still tried to figure out what to do with her life.

"Thank you." He moved along the house, pointing out gray ceilings, debris, missing panels and doors, torn-off molding, and so on.

Yeah, she'd be busy. Good. No time to think about what she'd done to end her marriage in disaster.

Her foot caught in debris, and she lost her balance. No! Her arms flailed, catching only air, and she was about to meet the dirty floor face-first. Greg snatched her forearm and steadied her.

Heat crept up her neck. Cullen had always ridiculed her for being accident-prone and had been especially furious when she'd once dropped a plate with a steak on an important dinner guest in their house.

You can't do anything right!

Her breathing faster, she regained her footing and peeked at Greg.

"Are you all right?"

Okay, so he didn't ridicule her for tripping around him for the second time but had caught her instead.

"Yes." Her skin tingled where he touched.

He towered over her, so she had to tilt her head back. His eyes were the aquamarine color of the ocean at Chapel Cove, so bright and gorgeous. He didn't let her go, though she could stand upright now.

And just like when she'd swam in the ocean, she felt light as she let the tide carry her away. A totally different tide threatened to carry her away now. She tried to say something but couldn't find her voice. Inhaling the woodsy scent of his cologne, she went lightheaded. His proximity wreaked havoc on her senses.

Something flashed in his eyes. Was it attraction? Or did she just want it to be?

Oh no.

What was she thinking?

She couldn't be attracted to a much younger man the day after her divorce, and her—okay, Roman's—client, could she? She'd be getting herself into a bigger mess than her foot was in.

Besides, she'd been deceived by a handsome face and an empty heart before.

"Thank you for catching me." Her voice sounded quiet, quieter than she'd intended.

Did his breathing increase like hers did, or was it her wishful thinking?

"You're welcome." He let her go, his expression changing to neutral. "Mr. Vela will be performing the work, correct?"

She passed the debris carefully. Well... She'd better give herself some wiggle room here. "I hope you won't mind if I'll be doing some of it."

"Actually, I'd prefer Mr. Vela to handle this. No offense, but I think it'll be easier for me to work with him."

What?

Her eyes widened.

So Greg was just like her ex—kindness itself in the beginning but diminishing her in subtle ways before gradually becoming worse. After seeing the way Greg had treated his daughter, she didn't expect him to be like that. But then, she knew very little about him besides the fact that he was a widower, a single father, and able to make her heart beat faster.

"Is it because I'm a woman?" Her small stature probably didn't help, either.

"I know many women work great in construction. But yes, I happen to think it'll be easier for a guy to perform some of these tasks."

Whoa.

She planted her palms on her hips. "Here's my phone number in case you change your mind." She rattled off the number.

Roman wasn't in any shape to perform repairs yet, at least, not in the scope Greg wanted. But her brother needed this job badly, both for his dignity and his pocketbook. Argh. She'd gladly give him what she'd managed to scrimp away from Cullen, but he wouldn't take it.

She pursed her lips. She had to help Roman. And she needed a paying job to gain confidence for future business.

What was she to do?

CHAPTER FOUR

AS SOON as Greg closed the door behind Kristina, his fingers itched to grab the phone and call her. Was he chauvinistic to ask her brother to do the repairs?

The reason wasn't that he didn't want her to do the work. The reason was that he wanted it a bit too much.

The spark of attraction was a betrayal of Sally's memory. How could he be so drawn to a stranger after recently meeting her? As he'd looked into Kristina's eyes when she'd nearly tripped and he'd steadied her, his heart, which he'd considered dead for romantic feelings, revved back to life.

But he'd loved and lost once, and pain still knifed him inside.

Besides, he couldn't be so selfish as to consider only his interests. His life revolved around his little girl. The less he saw of Kristina, the better off he'd be.

On the way to Chelsea's grandparents, the motor growled, and the air freshener gave a whiff of cherry, Sally's favorite scent. Even two years after her death, he still purchased the things she liked, used the same cologne as the one she'd given him for their first anniversary, and wore blue sweaters and T-shirts she'd bought for him because they'd matched his eyes.

As if it could somehow keep her present in his life... He still wore the wedding ring, though it was getting a little tight, and a similar painful band tightened around his lungs.

He called his former mother-in-law on his hands-free phone as he stopped at a traffic light. "Good evening, Mrs. Ronfrey. I'm on my way to pick up Chelsea."

"You're late."

At her brisk tone, he glanced at the dashboard. He was actually five minutes ahead of the agreed time, but experience promised arguing with Mrs. Ronfrey would be useless. He moved forward at the green light. "I had a meeting with Kristina Ve—"

"What? You're dating Kristina! You already forgot our daughter!"

He winced as her shrill voice ricocheted through the truck cab. "It wasn't a date. It was a business meeting. It's been two years since Sally died, but I haven't forgotten her." The vise constricted his heart, and he exhaled trying to release some pressure.

"*Only* two years! The business meeting. Right." Mrs. Ronfrey snorted. "You're seeing that Kristina woman. What kind of example are you showing your daughter? Oh, you don't care about Chelsea anymore. You just want to—"

"Please stop it," he said through his teeth as a surge of anger heated him. "I love Chelsea with all my heart. And I'm not seeing Kristina. It's..." The image of her dark, doe-like eyes appeared in front of him. "It's complicated. And didn't you say yourself she's trustworthy?"

"To take our grandchild to the restroom!" Mrs. Ronfrey exploded. "Not to replace our daughter in Chelsea's life!"

"Nobody is replacing anybody." He took a deep breath. This was his daughter's grandmother, and she needed her grandparents. He had to maintain a good relationship. "Chelsea adores Kristina. She's good to your granddaughter."

"Right! She's just trying to find a new husband and using our little girl for that." Mrs. Ronfrey's voice rose, irritating like grinding metal against glass. "No wonder you've been pawning off Chelsea on us while you're having fun."

He resisted the urge to grind his teeth as he made a turn. "I let Chelsea stay with you because you wanted so much to spend time with her."

"I see right through your lies. You chased women before marrying our daughter, and I knew it was a matter of time before you started doing it again."

Breathe in. Breathe out. Treat his former mother-in-law with respect, even if it wasn't easy. "I never claimed to be perfect, but there was nobody else in my life since I met Sally. There was nobody in my life for two years after her death."

The woman's snort reverberated down the line again. "You probably hid it well enough in Portland. But you can't hide in a small town. Think about your daughter. Think well. Otherwise, we'll do what we must." She disconnected.

Greg stared into space. His daughter occupied nearly all his thoughts already. And what was that threat "do what we must" about?

His heart dipped. Was even considering a relationship with Kristina too selfish?

He raked his fingers through his hair as he hooked another left. Then he rolled down the window. The cherry scent reminded him of Sally too much now, and ache in his chest grew. Nothing would bring Sally back.

Nothing.

Lord, why? We were so happy together.

Before Sally died, she'd asked him to lean on the Lord in his grief. Until her last breath, her faith had never wavered.

Greg's, however, had weakened a lot.

What had she said about people who hurt you? That he needed to pray for them. He couldn't pray for the Ronfreys. Not yet.

Lord, please give me the wisdom to build a good life for my little girl. And please help me not tell the Ronfreys off.

They are hurting, too.

The voice was quiet in his head, but it helped him understand them a little better.

As he neared Aileen's Pastries, the delicious aromas of freshly baked bread and brewed coffee reached him, bringing with them a totally different memory, a much more recent one. Sharing coffee with Kristina was a treat, in more ways than one. His heartbeat spiked more than he wanted.

He wasn't ready for a new start, and neither was his daughter. And he didn't like the veiled threat in Mrs. Ronfrey's voice when she said they'd do what they must.

Lord, please guide me. I want to do what's best for Chelsea. I really do. Please help my precious girl.

In the afternoon, Kristina strode along the shore and tugged tighter the jacket she'd thrown over her sweater. The breeze tenderly touched her skin as if trying to comfort a tired traveler after a long and difficult journey.

Her journey, however, had just begun.

As a teen, she used to love this place. Running along the shore with Reese and Nai, climbing the staircase in the lighthouse, staring into the vast ocean, laughing and dreaming big…

Now, how many of those dreams came true? Reese had become a supermodel and traveled the world. But now she was back in Chapel Cove, divorced and starting anew, as well.

As for Kristina, she still loved the Lord, but did she follow the path He'd chosen for her?

She breathed in fresh, salty air as seagulls cried loudly as if mocking her. She didn't particularly like the person she'd become, unsure of herself and even whiny, while she'd been so confident before. She'd gone the opposite way from Nai, who'd been shy at thirteen but grew into a confident woman who easily handled being a personal assistant to a billionaire.

As seagulls quieted, the waves' murmured as if trying to tell her something. She did have two wonderful children, and she didn't mind in the least that they both were girls, instead of having a boy and a girl.

Her heart squeezed painfully. Leanna still avoided her after divorce and didn't return her calls. Well, Reanna called regularly.

Should Kristina leave Leanna a voicemail, explaining Cullen was the one who filed for divorce? No, she didn't want to hurt the girls by ruining the image of their father.

She tipped her face to the sky. Where did the time go? When did her girls become grown-up and not needing her anymore, especially Leanna?

Seagulls screamed again as if they tried to answer, but she couldn't understand their language. Then she peered at her fist and slowly opened her fingers. Unlike the wedding ring she'd worn for nearly two decades, this new wedding ring didn't sparkle with diamonds.

A deep sigh left her lungs, and the wind carried it somewhere over the ocean.

Two months ago, Cullen said he needed to take her ring to readjust the insurance on it and had given her this one instead. According to him, the band was platinum. She'd known better, but when she'd opened her mouth to argue, her mother's screams rang in her ears. He'd never returned her real ring, and now she knew why.

His love for her had become as fake as this ring. Pressure built up in her chest, demanding release.

Dear Lord, please help me forgive Cullen. I don't want to carry this hatred. And please help Roman heal and Leanna talk to me again. In Jesus's name, amen.

She waved her arm and threw the ring as far as she could. Again, she took full lungs of humid, salty air and walked further down the beach.

Was Roman right, and instead of a disaster, this was the beginning of a new life?

Was God leading her on a new path?

She just needed to figure out what that path was. And for that, she needed to quieten her own self and listen to God.

For a few minutes, she strolled in silence.

Then she spotted a lonely figure, and something about it appeared familiar. Was this... Was this Greg Matthews?

His cyan-hued shirt was flapping in the breeze, a sharp contrast to his black slacks. Huh. A shirt wasn't nearly enough for this coast's low temperatures, but he didn't seem to notice.

He took something off his ring finger and kept it in his fist. A wedding ring? An expression of such profound sorrow etched his features that she took a step back. He closed his eyes and kissed his own fingers as if kissing the ring, and now, a deeper love than she'd ever seen on anybody's face mingled with his sorrow.

Even Cullen's face during their wedding didn't breathe this much love.

"Daddy! Daddy! Look at the seashell I found." Cute pigtails sticking out from under a pink knit hat, Chelsea ran to him, her little legs in tiny sparkling boots pumping fast.

He opened his eyes, his face lighting up with tenderness. Then he turned and threw the ring into the ocean, his expression pained.

The same gesture she'd done and what a difference...

As he scooped up the girl and whirled her around, Kristina stood motionless. She was heartbroken, yes, but she was free from abuse and offenses while Greg looked like he'd lost something profoundly precious.

Irreplaceable.

Her heart skipped a beat. She'd intruded on a private moment. She should leave.

"Miss Kristina!" Chelsea yelled, spotting her.

Well, it was too late to leave now.

Placing the girl on his shoulders, he strode to Kristina.

Her silly heart shifted in her chest. The guy didn't even want her to do work at his house. This embarrassing attraction must be one-sided. She steeled herself against the feeling growing in her chest.

His aquamarine eyes guarded, he nodded at her. "Good evening, Kristina."

"I knew we were gonna find you here!" Nothing guarded about Chelsea.

"Really?" Something warmed inside Kristina despite the breeze.

In the morning, she herself hadn't known she'd be coming to the ocean. But the ring felt so tight, and she wanted to get rid of it and all the baggage of insults and silent treatments. And she'd wanted to feel the salty breeze just like in childhood. Despite poverty and scandals at home, she'd been happy in this place while running around with the girls.

"Yeah. God told me to come here. When I prayed yesterday, I heard the ocean. Like in this seashell." The girl handed her a large seashell.

"Thank you." Kristina's fingers wrapped around the smooth surface.

Once upon a time, she'd had the same amazing faith. What had happened to it? Could she have it back?

Lord, please help me. And please help this precious child.

"I hope you weren't offended about the repair job." Was that guilt tightening Greg's voice as he walked beside her along the shore?

Wind threw her hair around her face, and she flipped it back with an impatient gesture. "Not at all." She did her best to keep her voice light. "After all, it stays in the family."

Stays in the family. She and Roman were twins. Different in stature, but Greg didn't know that.

Suddenly, she knew how to help her brother. Her heart started beating faster. Would she dare? Could she buy men's clothes larger in size to hide her feminine curves and men's shoes? If she could get a wig, a fake mustache and beard, and proper clothes, and learn to walk and talk like a man, this might work.

She nearly groaned. Her, posing as her brother? She had no clue how to behave like a man, and she was short to start with. It was ridiculous.

Lord, please guide me.

A loud exhale left his lungs. "I'm glad you look at it this way." His expression lightened somewhat. "Thank you for giving my daughter that toy. She adores Taco."

"Oh, Daddy!" Chelsea clapped her hands. "I know! I know! Miss Kristina can come with us to help me choose a puppy, right?"

He stopped in his tracks, then resumed his pace. "I don't recall anything about promising a puppy. Besides, it's not good for him to run in a small hotel room. We can't move into the house yet. And we really need to have our own place again." He turned to Kristina. "I'd love for your brother to start as soon as possible. Chelsea has a severe shellfish allergy, and the hotel here doesn't have rooms with kitchenettes. I don't like to get takeout because I'm afraid of cross-contamination with seafood."

Oh. Her twins had suffered from an egg allergy, and she'd experienced some scary times. Sympathy constricted her rib cage. "How do you manage then?"

"I have to cook at my former in-laws' kitchen." Judging by his frown, their relationship wasn't the best.

"Aw, Daddy! I wanna a puppy. Pretty-pretty please?" Chelsea stuck out the lower lip. She must be doing that gesture a lot.

Kristina hid a smile at Greg's helpless expression. Seeing a tall, muscular man at a loss for what to do with a child's request was kind of sweet.

Hmmm. She nibbled on her lower lip as she strolled beside them, the murmur of the ocean in the background. Maybe dressing up as Roman wasn't such a horrible idea. She obviously needed to get this little family into a new house fast. And in a small town, only a few people could do the job. Considering her brother's long time of medical issues, the other two guys were booked solid for a month ahead. She'd checked.

Was this the answer to her prayer?

Okay, tomorrow was Sunday, and she honored God and didn't work on Sundays. And she'd need a few days to figure out how to pull this off.

She took a deep breath for courage. "I talked to Roman, and he can start work Wednesday morning. Maybe at eight? Or is this too early?" She regretted the words even as they left her lips.

Oh man. What was she getting herself into? Greg would see right through her and hate her for lying to him.

He brightened. "Eight sounds great. I'll meet him at the house."

"He can do painting, fence mending, making a swing, things like that. He can hire out carpet installing." She considered Greg's obviously expensive clothes. "Unless you'd like hardwood floors."

"No, carpet would be more kid-friendly. Except for the living room, if possible."

"But not pet-friendly."

"What about my puppy?" Chelsea's eyes widened, and she blinked fast.

Oh no. The wail was coming.

Kristina had to think fast. "I rent a house, but the owner allows pets. I could keep the puppy while the repairs are being done. You could get a puppy sooner rather than later."

What? Why had she suggested this? Those baby blues must be affecting her judgment.

"Yay!" Chelsea clapped her tiny hands again. "Daddy, can we get the puppy now?"

He sent her a reproaching look. "We can't impose on Miss Kristina that much."

She sighed as she shook off sand from her shoes. She was getting deeper and deeper, and she didn't mean the sand. "Oops," she whispered to him. "Sorry about that."

A soft smile touched his lips like a ray of sunshine coming after clouds. "It's okay. With all her love for Taco, she could've asked for an elephant."

Chelsea's eyes widened. "I could have an elephant?"

As if realizing his slip, he groaned. "No! They are way too huge. And we'd have to move to Africa or India then."

"It's okay, Daddy. I like it here. And I like Grandpa, Grandma, and Miss Kristina." The girl giggled. "Now, down. I wanna find another seashell."

Greg brought Chelsea down from his shoulders and looked after her with enormous tenderness as her little feet patted the sand.

Something changed inside Kristina. Maybe he'd done her a favor by refusing her repair services. In a matter of days, she was getting attached to the small family.

The sun appeared from behind the clouds, and the water sparkled like a myriad of diamonds she owned once upon a time. The day was getting even better. She found herself smiling as she breathed deeply again.

Huh. She breathed better, slept better, ate better, and overall felt better without Cullen.

But did it mean she'd wasted over twenty years of her life on a man who wasn't worth it?

"Look, Daddy! I found another seashell!" Chelsea waved her treasure in the air.

"Good job, sweetie!" he yelled back.

Kristina smiled. "She's adorable. And she certainly loves her daddy, grandpa, and grandma."

His chuckle was without mirth. "Yeah. They love her, too. Can't stand me, though." He frowned. "I didn't mean to complain."

"Sometimes it helps to tell things to someone. Get them off your chest." Off his very broad chest. But she shouldn't be thinking that.

He picked up a pebble and threw it far in the ocean. "Maybe they are right. They think it's my fault Sally died. See, I used to be into extreme sports before I met Sally. I was making a name for myself in snowboarding. Not to brag, but a few of my videos went viral. But she was scared something might happen to me, so I gave all that up."

Peering at the ocean, he kept silent as if continuing was difficult for him.

Kristina touched his hand for support but jerked hers back immediately. "That was kind of you."

"That was nothing. I'd die for my wife. Sally had an MBA, and when we opened stores selling sports equipment, I did my best to make them successful. I was happy with her, very much so, especially after Chelsea was born. But a small part of me missed the adrenaline rush, and Sally guessed it. So for my birthday, she asked me to go snowboarding, to get the former thrill. I refused, but eventually, she talked me into it." His voice trembled, and a faraway look glazed his eyes as if he were staring beyond the horizon.

"Whatever happened next wasn't your fault," Kristina said quietly.

"The day I went to a ski resort, she went to get groceries. Thankfully, she left Chelsea with a babysitter. A drunken driver ran the red light. I rushed back as soon as I found out what happened. Sally lived for two more days, but the injuries were too severe. Her parents never forgave me, and neither have I." He closed his eyes as if the memories were too painful.

When he opened his eyes, so much suffering clouded them she couldn't help herself.

She snatched his hand. "No matter what your former in-laws say, it's not your fault Sally died. You couldn't have known."

He visibly swallowed. "I should've been there with her."

"Then both of you would've died. What would happen to Chelsea? Stop blaming yourself. Start living a new life. For yourself. For your daughter."

A muscle twitched in his jaw, but his fingers circled hers. "I'm trying. I've got to give Chelsea a good life. She deserves it."

"So do you," Kristina whispered as the warmth of his touch seemed to travel all the way to her heart.

"Look what I found!" Waving another seashell, the girl ran to them.

Reluctantly, Kristina let his hand go.

An invisible bond formed between her and Greg, a fragile one at first, and she didn't know whether she wanted it to grow stronger or needed to break it.

CHAPTER FIVE

TWO AND a half days later, Kristina lugged a heavy book box upstairs in the bookstore, Ivy's on Spruce. Her muscles strained, and sweat beaded her forehead.

Granted, she was still glad she'd phoned Reese the night before and suggested helping Nai get the place ready for her ailing aunt. After all, Nai grew too independent to ask for help. Besides, Kristina loved Nai's aunt Ivy, who'd always had a kind word, a good book, and a sweet pastry for them when they'd been kids. And now when Aunt Ivy had suffered a heart attack and couldn't climb to her room upstairs...

Compassion constricted Kristina's heart for the older woman as she plunked the hefty box on the floor and swiped sweat from her eyebrows. She breathed hard.

Of course, the familiar and oh-so-beloved place smelled like books, with a whiff of coffee and fresh pastries from the downstairs café. Bright lime-green interior walls contrasted the old Victorian's calmer moss-green exterior.

Sweet memories made her lips tug up. When she'd been little, she'd imagined this was a place from a fairy-tale, with its tower, bay window, and overall quirky appearance. It'd been wonderful to browse books, then munch on a delicious, fluffy pastry while chatting with the girls, the peaceful atmosphere so different from the shouts and scandals of her own place.

Huffing, Reese appeared with a large box. Tall, slim, blonde with a hint of red, and beautiful, her friend looked amazing and way younger than the big four-oh she was approaching.

Good thing Kristina loved her friend and didn't have an envious streak. Otherwise, she'd think life was unfair because all those tacos and fajitas always ended up on her hips. At least, according to Cullen. Argh. It was time to love her curves. Judging by Greg's words and the glances he had sent her way, he liked her just the way she was.

Warmth for a reason other than physical effort spread inside her. It was so important for a woman to be liked—or, even better, loved—the way she was.

No! No thinking about Greg. At least, not until she'd ask for girls' assistance to dress her up as her brother so she could do repairs at Greg's house. One good thing, Roman had agreed to help, after having a good laugh at her expense, of course.

She smiled at her lifelong friend. "Reese, you didn't change at all. Wow on being on those magazine covers."

Reese dropped the box on the floor. "Thanks. You look great yourself."

"Right." Kristina grimaced. "I can't say divorce agrees with me. It was heart-wrenching." Hmmm, but weren't her last years of marriage equally as painful, if not more?

"Tell me about it." A deep sigh left Reese's lungs.

Grunting, Nai appeared at the top of the stairs. Sure enough, she'd chosen a box bigger than the other women had.

"Let us help you with that," Kristina and Reese said in unison as they rushed forward and took the box from Nai's unwilling hands.

"I… could… do it myself." Nai huffed, short of breath. "But thanks."

They placed the box on the floor, and Nai hugged her friends, compassionate as ever. "I'm sorry you both had to go through painful divorces." She drew back, hands still on Kristina's shoulders and squeezed before releasing her. "Truly, Cullen's loss." Her fingers fisted. "I'd love to talk to that guy face-to-face."

"It's in the past." Kristina looked at Reese. "And sorry about Lloyd."

"Me, too." Nai frowned. "Looking at the two of you, I think maybe it's a good thing I dedicated my life to a career rather than marriage."

"Well, not all guys are like Cullen or Lloyd. Remember your childhood friend, Mateo Rodriguez? The one who just offered to help clear up the room for your aunt?" Kristina started. She wouldn't mind a second pair of hands, which actually were way more muscular than her own. Roman would've helped in a heartbeat, but he couldn't carry boxes while on crutches. "And you sent him away—"

Nai shot her a glare.

"Okay, never mind." Probably best to shut up.

Once upon a time, Mateo and Nai had spent so much time together, Kristina had hoped it could become something more than friendship. But after Mateo had stood Nai up for the junior prom…

Well, judging by Nai's sour expression, it was best not to talk about it.

Kristina rushed downstairs. "Come on, girls. Those boxes aren't going to move themselves."

"Huh. I recognize old, in-charge Kristina," Reese muttered behind her back.

For some time, between dragging books upstairs, they managed to catch up on all the events they didn't have time to go into detail about before. About Nai's life as a billionaire's assistant. About Reese's high-fashion career and recent divorce. About Kristina's raising twins and her marriage ending in disaster. Sure, they'd kept in touch via phone, texts, emails, video conferencing, but it wasn't the same as meeting like this.

Kristina's heart shifted. Only now she realized how much she'd missed the girls, their support and understanding.

Finally, the room downstairs didn't look like a storage room stuffed to the brim with books but like a place where someone could actually live.

Nai gave them a tight hug again. "Thank you so much, girls. What would I do without you?"

Reese and Kristina hugged her back, then eased out of the embrace.

Kristina shrugged. "Maybe then you'd have to accept help from—"

Another glare from Nai made Kristina clamp her mouth.

Oops. Hadn't she decided to keep her mouth shut about this? It didn't mean she'd give up on matchmaking, but she'd need a more subtle approach. A wonderful person like her bestie deserved happiness and true love.

Nai clapped her hands. "Now, let's have some coffee and pastries in the café. My treat."

A pleasant wave spread through Kristina. "Just like old times."

Nai and Reese nodded. "Just like old times."

Soon, they settled at the round alder table in a quiet corner of the café, steaming cups with freshly brewed coffee and warm, just-baked brioches in front of them.

"Who'll say grace?" Kristina looked around.

Silence was the answer. Her heart dipped. They'd all drifted away from God.

They should find their way back, and slowly, while she'd been healing after Cullen's betrayal, she'd been doing just that.

"I'll say grace." She took girls' hands and bowed her head. "Dear Heavenly Father, thank You for this food and please bless it. Please help us find our way to You again and help us heal. Please help Aunt Ivy recuperate as soon as possible. Please keep our beloved ones safe in Your care. And let us discover our own true selves, even at the age of forty. In the holy name of Your Son, Jesus Christ, amen."

"Amen," Reese and Nai echoed.

As Kristina savored the first bite of the brioche, she nearly purred. "Mmmm. This is such a great combination. The base of bread and all the scrumptious fillings. All the possibilities. Including my favorite, chocolate! Nai, you still remember."

Nai grinned as she sipped her coffee. "Of course. As well as the way you drink your coffee. One cream, no sugar. As for me, I decided to splurge and choose a brioche with caramel filling today."

After a few delicious bites, Kristina leaned forward. "Girls, I need your help. And advice. See, I met a man—"

"Excuse me." Nai blinked over the rim of her porcelain cup. "You just divorced, and you already met a man while I'm single forever and nobody showed up yet."

This time Kristina did a wise thing and didn't mention Nai's childhood friend who could've been much more than a friend by now if Nai had let him. Kristina wasn't entirely selfless. She did want a second brioche with chocolate filling.

"Nai, that's probably because you're too busy working and not looking for romance." Reese's amber eyes lit up. "Kristina, I'm curious to hear the details."

Kristina sipped her with-a-hint-of-caramel coffee, and it hit the spot. "Well, I met Greg before my divorce...."

The girls' eyes widened, and Nai nearly dropped her cup.

Uh-oh. Kristina caught herself. "No, don't get me wrong. It would never occur to me to cheat on Cullen, even after I found out about his infidelities. I met Greg in Chapel Cove last week... before the divorce was final. Really, there's nothing between us. We didn't even have a date." Warmth crept up her neck. "Well... First, I dropped his daughter's chocolate cake when we met. Then I fell into his arms. Oh, and I gave his daughter Taco."

Reese and Nai exchanged glances.

"Nai, do you understand anything?" Reese had wolfed down most of her dessert.

Nai shook her head, then nibbled a tiny bite of her brioche. Probably teenage memories of her mother criticizing her for gaining weight still affected her. "Nope. I think she ruined his daughter's cake, so she had to give her tacos to make up for it. Kristina, did you have dinner together? Hmmm, if it wasn't a date and there was nothing between you, why exactly did you fall into his arms?"

A good storyteller she was not. "Purely by accident." After a deep breath, Kristina related the events about meeting Greg and Chelsea. Somehow, she still managed to finish her brioche in the process.

When she was done, Nai sighed. "Wow. He must've loved his wife deeply. And poor Chelsea!"

"Doesn't mean he won't be capable of the same kind of love again." Reese took a few sips of her black coffee. "Did you say he's ten years your junior? Huh. Well, doesn't matter. Like I said, you look great."

"You don't sound too convincing." Kristina's heart sank.

"You do look lovely." Nai jumped to her feet. "Let me bring you another brioche. I know, with chocolate filling."

Nai disappeared in the direction of the counter and came back with a plate filled with brioches.

Kristina glanced at her hips, hesitated the moment, then grabbed the dessert and bit into the soft, warm, sweet deliciousness. "Anyway, I'm not interested in romance after two decades of Cullen's diminishing remarks. But I'm interested in a job. Greg bought a house in Chapel Cove that needs a lot of repairs, and he and Chelsea want to move in as soon as possible. The issue is, he decided to hire my brother, and there's no way Roman can do the work on crutches."

"Poor Roman." Sympathy flashed in Nai's eyes as she sipped her coffee.

"Yeah." Kristina finished the brioche way too soon again and sighed. Hmmm, how should she explain her idea? "So I need to become a man."

"Whoa." Reese's perfectly glossed lips rounded. "That's a drastic measure for a job, don't you think?"

Kristina held up a hand in a stop motion. "I meant I want to dress up as Roman. He needs a job badly with his medical bills piling up. And the family needs a house to move in." Her heart warmed. "Roman taught me how to do simple repairs when we were teenagers. And he said he'd teach me how to walk and talk like a man. I need your help putting the disguise on and getting it in the first place." The sweet chocolate filling soured in her stomach. "Or... It's a crazy idea, isn't it?"

Reese pursed those pink-glossed lips. "Yeah, a little. But from what I understood today, for twenty-two years you were obedient and submissive. It's about time you do something crazy, don't you think?"

Nai squared her shoulders as she thumped her cup onto the table. "Besides, it's rather chauvinistic of Greg not to hire you only because you are a woman. I've met with a similar attitude in the corporate world. I think you should do it. I'm game. I'll help you."

"Me, too." Reese took the second brioche. "Thankfully, there's a party shop in Chapel Cove. We should be able to get a disguise there—a wig, mustache, clothes, things like that."

Hope thudded Kristina's heart. Then she winced from a sting of guilt. "I hate lying to Greg. But this is the only way I see it can work. The other repair guys in Chapel Cove are booked solid."

Nai picked up her coffee cup. "Then it's decided. And I'll want to hear all the details later at one of our fortieth birthdays."

"Don't remind me." Kristina grimaced, then drained her coffee to the last drop to sweeten the bitter taste. "I think I'll just celebrate a thirty-ninth birthday again and keep celebrating this way for the next ten years. No, make it the next twenty years."

Nai sent her an encouraging smile as she took another tiny bite of her brioche. "You look only twenty-nine. Or even twenty-eight. And you caught the attention of a much younger man, which can become something more. Maybe even love. Your daughters are grown-up and doing great. And you're starting a new exciting career in your hometown where people remember and love you. A good beginning."

Her chest expanding, Kristina nodded. "I hope so. God is good."

Nai paused, then gave an uncertain. "Amen to that."

Just a few days ago, Kristina had seen herself as a failure, but one chance meeting had changed it all.

Could she hope that God had sent her Greg and Chelsea for a reason?

Could she build new happiness on the ruins of unhappiness, after all?

The next morning, Greg leaped past debris to answer the knock on the door. He glanced at his watch. Eight o'clock sharp.

He flung the door open and froze.

Standing on the porch, Roman Vela was short. Very short. Probably about Kristina's height. Didn't look too muscular, either. Greg nearly cringed, having a hard time imagining this guy lifting heavy paint cans and instruments.

Dressed in baggy gray overalls with a cap drawn low, both spackled with paint, the guy kept his hands in his pockets. Some similar features to his twin sister lurked behind his dark mustache and beard.

Greg frowned. That's what he got for refusing Kristina's help. But he was attracted enough to that woman already. No need to risk seeing her daily.

Ironing out his frown, Greg managed a welcoming smile. "Come on in. I'm Greg Matthews. Please call me Greg."

The guy stepped inside. "I'm Roman Vela. Call me Roman, please." His gruff voice sounded strange. "I brought ceiling paint in the truck and the samples of interior paints for the walls my sister said you wanted."

"Thank you." Rubbing the back of his neck, Greg sized the man up. Maybe he should've hired a crew, even if he had to request it from Portland.

Roman squared his shoulders. "I know I'm not tall and muscular. But I get the job done."

And his reviews attested to the statement. Letting his hand lower from his neck, Greg nodded. "Let's start then. I'll help."

It wouldn't hurt to give the man a chance. Besides, Greg needed a suitable house. Looking for the crew would postpone matters. If this Vela wasn't capable, he'd deal with it then.

Greg followed Roman to the truck, which had a tall ladder, toolboxes, wire, and a few pails. Greg grabbed one of the large pails of ceiling paint. A vein bulged on Roman's forehead as he lifted another pail with both hands.

Yeah, this was going to be a long day.

"Let me help you with that." Greg grasped the handle.

Roman hesitated, then stepped aside, letting go. He picked up a tray with two white covers, two rollers, and a pack of roller covers. After they dropped everything in the living room, he turned to Greg. "I'll bring a pack of large trash bags and a ladder."

Greg followed him. "I'll give you a hand with a ladder."

"I can handle it." Roman didn't sound too sure.

If the man collapsed under the weight, Greg would have to do the job alone. Well, until he could find someone else. So he might as well get to the ladder first.

He rushed outside, passed the guy, and grabbed the cold metallic surface. "I've got it."

Roman opened his mouth as if to argue, but a whoosh of relief beat any words out. "Thanks, man."

Greg's muscles bulged as he dragged the ladder inside. How did the poor guy carry this thing on a regular basis? A mystery.

After Greg placed the ladder against the wall, Roman handed him a pair of rubber gloves and a few trash bags. "If you're still up to helping, I think we need to clean up here first. But I truly don't mind doing it all by myself."

If Chelsea's grandparents hadn't taken her again and told him not to show up before the evening, he might've agreed. But in this case… "I'm not afraid to get dirty. I want to give Chelsea that room with purple elephants as soon as I can."

Something flashed in Roman's eyes. Respect? Admiration? "You're a great father."

Greg swallowed hard. "I hope I'm at least a *good* father. But I don't know how to be a father and a mother at the same time."

"Just trust in God. And do your best." Roman's voice softened.

Once upon a time, Greg had trusted God with his whole heart, after Sally, a true Christian, had led him to the Lord. But that had been before Sally died.

His heart heavy, Greg snapped rubber gloves on and busied himself with work. Without discussing it, he and Roman went to separate rooms. In about an hour, they finished taking out the trash and debris.

The front door squeaked as Roman came back with a stack of newspapers. "Though we're going to redo floors, this will leave less mess. What room would you like to start with?"

He didn't hesitate. "Chelsea's room." That was a priority.

"Sounds good." Roman smiled.

That smile reminded Greg of Kristina.

He couldn't explain it, but he wanted to see her. Just talking to her, seeing that smile, and feeling her compassion made the pain lessen and something akin to hope blossom instead. He felt an incredible pull toward that woman.

Not good.

Shaking his head free of the memory, he took half of the newspapers and started spreading them over Chelsea's bedroom floor while Roman did the same.

"Do you know if your sister is seeing anyone?" Greg stilled, the sheet of paper nearly escaping from his hands. Why was he asking this? He shouldn't. And there was no reason for his heart to beat faster.

Yes, she'd just divorced, but an attractive woman like that could have a new man in her life quickly.

Roman's eyes widened, and he coughed a little. "Not that I know of. Um, why are you asking?"

"No reason at all." Hope expanded inside him as he finished laying the newspaper. It shouldn't matter if Kristina was available.

Roman retrieved two pairs of protective glasses and a cap. He handed over one pair and the gray cap. "Otherwise, you'll be covered in the ceiling paint."

As Greg put them on, the guy nudged him in the forearm. "If you're interested in her at any level, I need to know if *you're* seeing anyone. Well, as her brother. You get it, right?"

This conversation was getting too personal, but he'd started it. "I understand. No, I'm not seeing anyone."

"Good. Do you think of asking her out?" Roman's tone was teasing, but Greg sensed apprehension in it as if the answer mattered to him a lot. He really seemed to care about his sister, but then they said twins were close.

"I'd like to spend more time with her, but I don't want to produce the wrong impression. I'm not looking for romance. I loved Chelsea's mother too much to risk that kind of heartache again. So it might be wrong to ask Kristina to dinner when I'm not looking for a date."

"Oh. I see. I'm very sorry for your loss." Sadness shadowed Roman's eyes. "Well, after her disastrous marriage, my sister isn't looking for romance, either. You both need an ally, a friend to help you transition to a new stage in life. Maybe you can be such a person for each other."

Now something more than hope swelled in Greg's chest. Tenderness? Excitement to see Kristina again? His pulse spiked too much for a prospect of something that wasn't even a date.

Though, for some reason, the fact that she wasn't looking for romance irked him instead of being a relief.

"Thanks, man. Your approval means a lot to me. I heard Latino families are pretty tight." He gave Roman a pat on the shoulder.

The pat wasn't even that strong, but the guy nearly lurched forward.

"Any time." Roman rubbed his shoulder. "And yep, we are."

They retrieved the paint tools, paint, and ladder from the main room.

Excitement building up, Greg put the heavy ladder on Chelsea's room floor. He couldn't wait to hear Kristina's voice. "I'll call her right now."

The roller slipped from Roman's hands and thumped on the floor. "No!" His voice rose strangely. He coughed again. "I mean, look, man, we have our hands full here. First things first. Let's finish painting the ceiling, and then feel free to call her. After I leave."

Strange. Well, maybe the guy didn't want to intrude on a private conversation.

"Okay." Greg could respect that. He stifled disappointment over waiting hours.

A stab of guilt reminded him he needed to think of Chelsea's interests before his own. Maybe he could take Chelsea to dinner with them. He'd call the restaurant in advance to make sure no shellfish was in her order and remind the server about it, too.

Kristina had seemed like an attentive woman, so she wouldn't choose a restaurant that served seafood, knowing about his girl's allergy.

"You're not going to forget to call her, right?" Roman removed plastic from two roller covers and fit covers on rollers. He handed Greg one, and then the extension handle, too.

How could he forget when she invaded his thoughts now? Greg placed the roller on the extension handle. "No."

"Okay, but I'll remind you, just in case." The guy marched to the ladder and climbed it.

After a few minutes of moving the roller along the ceiling, Greg said, "I can't believe your sister's husband treated her the way he did. When she told me about it, I felt like punching the jerk."

Roman chuckled atop the ladder. "You sound like my brother."

"You and Kristina have another sibling?" Hopefully, the other brother would be as open to Greg's "occasionally meeting his sister for dinner" as this guy was.

The roller in Roman's hands stopped moving. "Did I say brother? I meant cousin. He's very protective of Kristina."

"He wouldn't object to me dating her?" Now it was Greg's turn to cough. Oops. "I meant meeting her for dinner? I don't want to cause her any family issues." His heart shifting in his chest told him he didn't want to give up on the idea of seeing her, either.

"Nah." Roman resumed painting. "While we care about her, we let her make her own decisions. Not that she'd allow us to interfere, either."

"I kind of regret not hiring your sister." He might as well get it off his chest.

Roman moved so fast the ladder shook. "You do?"

Greg placed the roller cover in the paint tray and steadied the ladder.

Then he stepped back and resumed painting the ceiling, thankful for his height and the extension handle. He didn't trust those ladders. "I didn't mean to offend her. I just didn't want her to do rigorous physical labor. And, well, there was another reason. I hope she doesn't hold a grudge."

"I can tell you my sister's not a type to hold a grudge." A cheerful lilt eased the gruffness in Roman's voice.

Greg smiled. "I got the same impression, but I figured I'd ask."

For some time, they worked in silence. Then Roman glanced back from the ladder. "It's nice of you to be moving to Chapel Cove so Chelsea can be closer to her grandparents."

"They adore her. Wish I could take her closer to my parents, as well." Wistfulness tightened his lungs. "But after retiring, they moved to England, and for the most part, they're not up to traveling. I took Chelsea to England to see them a few times, but I don't want her to go through a long international trip too often. And I'm always afraid she could get an anaphylactic shock from possible cross-contamination with seafood in the meals."

"It's wise of you to be careful," Roman said quietly.

Then Greg's heart warmed. "I thought my marriage would be like my parents' marriage. They've been together for over half a century and are still very much in love."

For some reason, Kristina's image stood in front of him. Could he have another chance at the forever kind of love? Or would it be too much to hope for? Some people never met their soulmate, and he'd already had one in Sally.

"Wow. That's awesome. My parents' marriage was the opposite." His voice sad, Roman continued painting the ceiling. "There were constant scandals when I was growing up, mostly started by Mom. When I was fourteen, Dad seemed to have enough. He divorced her and moved to Paraguay where his ancestors were from. And every time he flew back to Oregon to see us, Mom found an excuse not to let it happen. We missed him so much. For years, she told us he forgot all about us until we started wondering whether that could be true."

Greg's hand stopped moving. "That must've been tough. Might be one of the reasons Kristina stayed married to a jerk for so long. She didn't want her children to be without their father after knowing first-hand how difficult it was."

Roman nodded. "You're right."

How a man could mistreat a compassionate, caring woman like .
Kristina was beyond Greg. He resumed painting.

When they finished the ceiling in Chelsea's room, Greg,
Roman, and the paint tools moved to the living room, then to one
of the bedrooms and the hall.

While they worked, Roman told him about the church he went
to, a few great places to eat in town, like The Pancake Shoppe on
the boardwalk that surely didn't have seafood, the park on the
outskirts that would be good for Chelsea, and the lavender farm
she might like to visit one day. Greg filed that information in his
head and added directions to Ivy's on Spruce, a bookstore that was
a great source of children's books. Ivy's on Spruce also served
fabulous brioches, including ones with chocolate filling.

Greg smiled. His daughter and Kristina shared a love for
chocolate, so Chelsea would definitely be thrilled to try those
chocolate-filled brioches. Then Roman told him how to drive to
Paws and Whiskers, an animal shelter. Also useful information,
considering his daughter's requests for a puppy were getting more
and more insistent. There was apparently an amusement park in
town, too. It was incredible how Roman seemed to read Greg's
mind and gave him exactly the information he needed.

Roman turned out to be a good guy, and Greg cringed over his
earlier attitude. He dipped the roller cover in paint, then took a
deep breath determined to ask a few questions about the person
who interested him much more than he wanted to admit. "What
kind of food does Kristina like?"

"Mexican food like tacos, tamales, fajitas, barbacoa,
guacamole."

Greg rolled the cover along the tray, gathering paint.
Thankfully, Sally had taught him how to make tacos. Maybe one
day, when he moved into this place, he could—

Hold on. Thoughts about Sally hadn't occupied his mind as they used to, and now when they appeared, they didn't bring the same sharp pain. He didn't want to forget her, but...

Lord, does it mean I'm on the way to healing?

Could Sally be right and God heard all the prayers?

Greg resumed painting the ceiling. "Do you have a Mexican restaurant here that you'd recommend?"

"Sure. Tía Irma's." Roman rattled off the address.

Greg wanted to know more about Kristina, her likes and dislikes, and how to take the sadness away from her dark eyes. But he'd probably best not push it further.

By the time they finished, his muscles ached from holding his arms above him. How did Roman do this on a regular basis?

And he needed to have lots of energy because he wanted to take Chelsea to the shelter for a puppy after he picked her up.

"I'll just leave the ladder and the paint tools here for tomorrow." Roman, his face—including mustache and beard—covered with tiny white specks, surveyed the work.

"Sure. Um, do you think your sister will join me and Chelsea to go choose a puppy for my daughter at Paws and Whiskers?"

Roman didn't hesitate. "She'll be happy to." He must really know his twin well.

As soon as the door closed behind Roman, Greg fished out his phone from the back pocket of his jeans, eager to hear her voice.

What was it about Kristina that made him want to talk to her so much?

CHAPTER SIX

KRISTINA SPRINTED to Roman's truck from Greg's house and jumped inside it. As soon as she turned the key in the ignition and the motor revved to life, her phone rang.

Yes! She made it in time. She'd been so scared Greg would call before she left and the phone ringing in her pocket would give her away.

Her heart skipped a beat as she said hello. Her voice came rougher than usual due to hours trying to talk like a guy.

Oops. "Hello," she repeated in her regular voice.

A whiff of the green-apple scent of the car air freshener drifted to her, but all she could think about was Greg's woodsy cologne and smoldering eyes.

"Hello, Kristina. I was wondering if you'd agree to go pick a puppy for Chelsea with us tonight." His voice sounded hopeful.

Her arm muscles, hurting like never before, screamed at her to answer no. "Of course."

Despite her muscles groaning, her lips tugged up. And the reason she agreed to it wasn't because he made her pulse skyrocket and she couldn't wait to see him. Well, to see him as herself, Kristina. It took a lot of effort to avoid looking at him and hide her affection in the few times she'd stolen glances. The reason she'd agreed was because she wanted to help the little girl.

Okay, that, too.

"Great!" His enthusiasm made her smile widen. "And... would you like to have dinner with me and Chelsea tomorrow?"

Though she knew this was coming, her pulse spiked. "Of course." Argh. She was repeating words like a parrot. "I mean, I'd love to." Here, this was better.

"Awesome. I'll see you in an hour."

She winced. "What? An hour?"

Really?

Her mind whirled. The distance to her rental was small, but... She only had an hour to drive home, peel the facial hair off her face, take a shower, scrub ceiling paint from her skin, do makeup and hair, and find something to wear to appeal to a much younger man—all with aching arms and a racing heart?

Um, not that she should be trying to appeal to him, but she couldn't quite meet him wearing a mustache and beard, could she?

"Would that be okay?" A slight strain—only noticeable because she'd spent the last hours getting to know his reactions—tightened his voice. "We want to make it to the animal shelter before they close."

"Of course," she squeaked again.

She peeled off from the curb.

She'd never driven as fast or parked as quickly. She dashed straight for the shower and ripped off her clothes. Ripping off facial hair was a different matter.

"Ouch! Ouch! Ouch!" Finally, that was done.

Putting the disguise on was so much more fun than getting rid of it. Not to mention she'd had Nai's help while trying to make herself look like a man. What a great friend Nai was, to get to Kristina's house at seven in the morning after a tiring day of moving boxes and managing the bookstore!

Argh. Getting rid of the beard and mustache was still much easier than removing all the white ceiling paint dotting her skin. Covered in paint wasn't the way she wanted to look for her first date after divorce.

She rubbed herself dry furiously. Not that this was a date. Not at all.

Wrapping a soft bathrobe, she cringed. Her hair hung flat after wearing the wig all day.

Great.

Not!

No time to wash and style it. She brushed her hair fast as she hurried to her closet. Then she stopped in her tracks. The eternal question of all females plagued her.

What to wear?

It might've been easier to answer it in the times when the only option was an assortment of animal skins.

If Cullen, who was her own age, hated her clothing style and wasn't shy about voicing it, what about a man ten years her junior?

She pulled her shoulders back. Okay, a friend to the rescue. Reese? Well, as a fashion expert, Reese would probably give her too many ideas, setting Kristina back to square one. Nai!

Kristina rushed back to the living room, dropped the hairbrush on the coffee table, found her phone, and called Nai.

"I have an emergency," she said as soon as her friend answered.

"What happened?"

Cringing at Nai's alarmed voice, Kristina lowered herself on the couch. "I'm going to see Greg in about"—she looked at her watch—"seven minutes, and I have no clue what to wear."

"Oh, that kind of emergency. Go get that man."

"Nai! It's not a date." She nearly groaned.

Nai snorted. "Right. Are you going to a fancy restaurant?"

As if her friend could see her, she shook her head vigorously. She was fed up with fancy restaurants after all Cullen's business dinners with clients where she'd had to smile, answer politely, and act like the perfect wife of an important person. "Nope. We're going to the animal shelter to get a puppy for his daughter."

"I guess a stunning evening gown is out then." Nai chuckled.

"You're supposed to be helping me!" A glance at her watch had her heading back to the closet. Her arms felt filled with lead. "Well, now I have only five minutes, thank you very much. And I don't even have the makeup on yet. I spent the whole day painting ceilings with him and didn't have time to prepare and—"

"Painting ceilings, huh?" Nai sounded way too cheerful for such a serious matter. "He sounds like a down-to-earth guy. How about blue jeans, a light sweater, and some kind of jacket?"

Once in the closet, Kristina examined her clothes. "Okay, I have a few pairs of jeans."

"A little hint. Not the baggy kind. You've got curves. Don't be afraid to show them."

"I wish I had your confidence." Kristina put Nai on the speakerphone and placed the phone on the shelf while she wiggled into *fitting* blue jeans. "I've got a small black turtleneck. But I only have a white jacket. And tall white boots Reanna gave me for my birthday. I never wore the jacket and boots. Cullen said white made me look fat."

"Cullen is a jerk. Forget what he said! You're gorgeous and slim, with curves in the right places. Put on that white jacket and boots and a beautiful smile and go get him."

Kristina pulled on the sweater. "Didn't I just say—"

Nai laughed. "By go get him, I meant the puppy. Who do you think I was talking about?"

"You're a great friend." Kristina shrugged into a white jacket.

"Ditto. Um, you mentioned you didn't have a chance to put on makeup. So just a friendly reminder to check that you took off your *entire* disguise and no tiny patches of facial hair left. Don't get me wrong, I don't mind you wearing a beard and a mustache. But something tells me they might not be in Greg's taste. Just a hunch."

"Oh no! Bye, Nai!" She dashed to the bathroom just as the doorbell chimed outside.

How did he end up in this predicament?

Greg stole a glance at Kristina's lovely profile as he drove to her house.

Two pets instead of one. And if it were up to his daughter, they'd be driving back with all the animals from the shelter right now.

"It's okay. I can keep the puppy while you have the kitten in the hotel." Kristina seemed to read his thoughts. "We... um, I mean, my brother and you are already almost done with the ceilings. Painting walls inside shouldn't take long. You should be able to move in soon enough."

Kristina was a godsend.

Gratitude and something else, what he didn't dare to name yet, filled his chest.

"Cupcake and I are gonna have our room with purple elephants?" Chelsea said from the backseat.

"Of course, sweetie." Kristina's voice warmed as she turned back. "Cupcake?"

In the rearview mirror, he could see his child hugging the brownish-black kitten, a huge grin on her dear face. "Yes. This is Cupcake."

He and Kristina exchanged knowing glances, remembering delicious cupcakes they'd shared.

"What do you want to name the puppy?" Kristina lifted the tiny dachshund, dappled with chocolate and tan spots around the strikingly blue eyes, floppy ears, and large front paws.

From what he knew, medium-sized dachshunds were bred to chase badgers and other furrow-dwelling animals, but his child would never use the dog for that. The only danger any animal had in Chelsea's presence was to be hugged to death.

"Hmmm, the name. Chocolate Chip Cookie. Cookie for short," the girl said with authority.

There was a pause.

Hmmm. After making a turn, he glanced at Kristina as she stared at the little canine. Ah, now he understood the reason for her pause.

"Um, sweetie…" An adorable blush colored Kristina's face. "I think Cookie is better suited for a girl. We have a boy here."

His daughter didn't let such a small detail affect her. "Then it's going to be Chocolate Chip. Chip for short."

He couldn't help a chuckle as he made a turn. "Works for me." He slightly leaned toward Kristina. "Thank you."

"My pleasure." Her voice dipped to a barely audible whisper. "I hope you're not upset about getting two pets instead of one. At least, we talked her out of a ferret."

He actually didn't mind a ferret. He happened to like ferrets, as well as turtles, squirrels, parrots, and many breeds of dogs and cats. But three pets were going to be an overkill, especially until they could move into a house.

"Daddy, we had to get Chip. How can you resist those eyes?"

He looked back at his child's baby blues before returning his attention to the road. "Really, how could I resist those eyes?"

Then he looked at Kristina and thought the same thing.

In the morning, the shrilling alarm jerked Kristina out of the dreamland. She groaned and pressed snooze. She'd just hurry up while getting ready.

A few more times of pressing the snooze button later, she flung open her eyes. What? She sat up in bed and gawked at her watch. Seven thirty. It couldn't be *that* late already! She had very little time left to put on her disguise and reach Greg's house.

No, no, no. She grabbed her phone and called him.

"Good morning, Kristina." Just his voice made her heart flutter.

Remember to be professional.

"Roman called me. He's, um, running late. He's apologizing. A lot." She leaped out of her bed, and her bare feet touched the cold tile.

Ouch!

"So that's the reason you're calling me." Disappointment dulled his voice.

She wanted so badly to talk to him, hear his voice…. But she had to hurry. She slid her feet into soft slippers and dashed to the bathroom. "That, and to say I look forward to seeing you at dinner tonight."

"Me, too." His voice turned husky.

So not fair she had to hang up on him. She could listen to that voice forever. "I have to go. Sorry." She disconnected.

As she brushed her teeth, the minty toothpaste refreshing her mouth, a nagging feeling she was forgetting something wasn't leaving her.

What was it?

Oh, the puppy!

She rinsed her mouth and hurried to her living room. The dog's bed she'd bought for Chip was empty.

"Chip! Chip, where are you?" Calling out, she went through her rooms. She even checked all the drawers.

Nothing. She stifled her disappointment.

Okay, maybe he'd come to food. She sprinted to her kitchen, put the contents of the pet food can into a bowl, and placed it on the floor. "Chip, I have something yummy for you!"

A few moments later, Chip still didn't arrive. Well, well, well. She couldn't wait much longer. She needed to start working. Cringing, she hurried to the bedroom, grabbed her cell phone from the nightstand, and called her brother.

"*Hola, hermano.* I need your help. Can you take care of Chip while I work at Greg's place, please?" Well, whenever she found the puppy, that was.

There was a pause. "You want me to take care of a computer chip?"

She really didn't have time for this. She put the phone on the speakerphone, placed it on the floor, and dropped on her stomach on the cold tile. Nope, the pup wasn't under her bed, either. "More like Chocolate Chip. Well, he was a Cookie first."

"You worry me, hermanita. Did you fall from my ladder and hit your head? You want me to take care of a chocolate chip cookie? Why?"

Oookay. She needed to start again, slower this time. "It's a puppy. Greg and Chelsea's new puppy. I volunteered to take care of the pet while they were living in the hotel. But I don't want to leave him by himself. I'd hate for him to be alone in an unknown place. He's not even housebroken yet. Help me. *Por favor.*"

Another pause. Usually, they understood each other way better than that. She turned the bedspread to make her bed. Chip was sleeping sweetly under the cover.

She squealed.

"Was that you or the puppy?" Roman chuckled.

"Me. So are you going to help me?" She grabbed the dog, his fur smooth under her fingertips.

Chip opened his eyes, yawned, and stretched.

"Not to mention, he could chew the furniture and make puddles. Sure. He'll keep me company."

"Ay, *gracias.*"

"No need to thank me. You're doing a lot for me, too." He paused again. "And I mean this in the best way possible, but how is your mustache?"

Her hand flew to her face. "Oh no. I forgot my disguise." As another of Roman's chuckles traveled down the line, she frowned. "You're enjoying this, aren't you?"

"Hey, I wasn't the one who came up with the idea to impersonate me. But now you have an image to uphold. Make it good. I'll grab my laptop, take a cab, and be at your place in a jiffy."

"*Muchissimas gracias.* Okay, gotta go." She disconnected and rushed to the kitchen where she fed half-asleep Chip.

Putting on the disguise took her longer than the day before, so when her doorbell rang, she snatched her wig, pulled it on, and darted to open the door.

Crutches clicking against the tile, Roman walked inside. Barking, Chip ran to the door, slipped on the tile, fell on his behind, thought about something, then got up, and started barking again.

She stooped to the puppy and patted him. "Chip, this is my brother. Treat him well." She straightened out. "Cans with puppy food are in the kitchen cabinet near the sink. Also, make sure he has water. And—"

"Got it. By the way, the right side of your mustache peeled off. On the other hand, your beard looks great." Roman kept a straight face for a moment, then started laughing. "I never thought I'd say such things to my hermanita."

She groaned and tried to fix her mustache while Roman scooped Chip up. "Thanks. I think." She slid her feet in black men's shoes a few sizes too big. Stuffing them with newspapers and wearing two pairs of socks could only help so much.

A sting of guilt made her wince. She didn't like to deceive Greg, and the more she knew him, the guiltier she felt. She should fess up. But risk seeing disappointment in his eyes? Also, risk her brother's professional reputation?

"I need to finish this charade." How, she didn't know yet.

"Nah. We're having way too much fun here." Roman jostled the puppy. "Right, Chip?"

Chip, the traitor, barked his agreement.

About fifteen minutes later, after a mad dash from her brother's truck to Greg's porch, Kristina breathed deeply of air filled with the scents of grass and foliage.

Greg was so not going to be happy with her being this late. Correction. He wasn't going to be happy with her brother. She cringed. How had she gotten herself into this mess? She really needed to tell him the truth. At the right moment.

Lord, please forgive me for lying to Greg.

He opened the door and waved her in. "Good morning." Judging by the smile, he wasn't angry at all.

Huh. She scooted inside and stopped in her tracks. She'd never particularly liked gray, but this light shade appeared elegant and fresh. So, the living room walls were painted already. She stole a glance at him. Pink dots decorated his white T-shirt and cap alongside the gray ones. Apparently, Chelsea's room was painted, too.

Her cheeks flamed up in embarrassment. "I'm sorry I'm late." And then her face flamed for a different reason as she stared at his biceps—his exceptionally well-built biceps.

Oh no, look away fast! She shouldn't be salivating over his muscles as Kristina, much less as Roman. And she shouldn't be blushing, either.

Thankfully, he was looking at the work he'd done.

"It's okay. I couldn't sleep, so I started early. Chelsea's grandparents insisted on seeing her in the evening, and she fell asleep there. They begged me not to wake her up and leave her overnight and today. The hotel room felt so empty without her." He grimaced, probably having missed his little girl, then lifted the arctic-blue paint pail like it weighed nothing. Well, okay, his biceps bulged a little.

Don't look!

She was behaving like a hormone-struck teenage girl when she was supposed to be a forty-year-old man.

Maybe paint vapors were getting to her. Only she hadn't breathed any yet.

"I'm going to paint the guest bedroom. Chelsea wanted it this shade of blue. Are you coming?" He threw the words over his shoulder. Over his *broad* shoulder.

What was going on with her?

She cringed. She shouldn't be in the same room with him for long, or she'd give herself away.

"Um, I'm going to work on those purple elephants." She reached for the pencil in her bag. She'd had the presence of mind to bring it.

"Good idea. I can't draw to save my life." He marched to the guest bedroom.

She hurried to Chelsea's room where she started sketching three elephants on one wall. Dad, Mom, and a baby elephant. He'd obviously painted this room first and had started extremely early for the paint to be nearly dry to touch.

While her pencil moved, her mind whirled. Okay, it wasn't just Greg's spectacular muscles that attracted her or his youth or his chiseled features, though she certainly wasn't complaining. It was the way he cared about his daughter, the lingering sadness in his aquamarine eyes she so badly wanted to erase, and how he talked about his late wife that showed he could love with his whole heart.

But was there any love left there for her then? Her stomach tightened. She must be a sucker for punishment to be falling for a guy whose heart wasn't available.

After finishing sketching the small elephant family, she stepped back. She smiled. Okay, looking good.

Then she made a trip to the living room, brought purple paint and paint brushes, and started filling in the contours. Soon two elephants joined the first family, one grazing in the field, another one washing in the lake. She even threw in a giraffe, purple, of course. Maybe Chelsea would like it.

She'd worked so fast, and so much joy spread inside her as if she'd been born to do this. Maybe the Lord was telling her something right now.

"Great job." Greg's voice made her whirl around. "Chelsea is going to love this."

"Thank you. I hope so." She did her best to keep her voice rough.

She looked at him, and just like that, her heartbeat went into overdrive. She forced herself to turn away. Every day, she was getting more and more attracted. She wasn't going to last long as Roman Vela. Not at all.

Greg frowned as if he were going to say something unpleasant. "I need to talk to you."

Her heart dropped. Here we go. He figured her out already. But if not, she needed to behave like a man. Not a woman who wanted to wrap her arms around Greg's neck and kiss him…

Not helping!

She shoved her hands into her pockets. "Yeah?" At least, her voice sounded rough enough.

"I like what you did here." He gestured to the wall. "But would you mind if your sister finishes the work? I kinda feel bad not giving her the job in the first place. That is, if she's okay working long hours."

She barely resisted the urge to squeal. Squealing would've ruined everything. "Huh. Sure. I don't mind. It stays in the family. I'll tell Kristina. She'll be thrilled, long hours and all."

His expression softened. "You're a great sibling."

She coughed a little. "I love Kristina as much as I love myself." And wasn't that the truth.

"One thing, though." He raked his fingers through his hair. "Chelsea wanted a swing. Maybe it would be easier if you make it today instead of Kristina."

"Okay. Let's work on the tree swing." Grateful her brother had taught her how to make those in high school, she chose her next words carefully. "But I can honestly say Kristina and I have about the same amount of knowledge on building a swing or doing repairs."

"She sounds like an amazing woman. Beautiful, hardworking, patient. But she seems unaware of her great qualities, even unsure of herself sometimes. I hope one day she'll meet a great man who'll value her true worth." A strange expression flashed in his aquamarine eyes.

Her heart shifted. The thing was, she'd already met the man she wanted to value her true worth. A man who'd loved and lost and wasn't ready to love again.

He was standing right in front of her, and she didn't even dare to look at him.

Love Me

.

CHAPTER SEVEN

WAITING FOR Kristina in the evening, Greg settled in the booth at Tía Irma's. He'd never been to the place with clay pots on the shelves and scenes from artisan lives hand-painted on the walls. Everything was colorful from mustard-hued walls to scarlet salsa bottles on every table and pear-green skirts on the waitresses.

Hopefully, the food would be good. If Kristina liked it, he was game. And her brother said she liked it.

Hmmm. Roman Vela was strange. But he worked hard and loved his family, and that was what mattered. A few times Greg had an impression Roman pretended to be somebody else. His hands were rather small and gentle for a guy working in the home repair business and reminded him of Kristina's. And the gait wasn't exactly manly.

Could it be?

Greg pushed away his doubts.

His heart skipped a beat in the anticipation of Kristina's arrival. Meanwhile, his mouth watered at the delicious scents of beef fajitas and *caldo de res* when a waiter passed by, carrying a tray for somebody else.

His foot tapping against the worn-out Mexican tile, he checked his watch. Shouldn't she be here already? What if she changed her mind? His lips pressed tight.

"She'll be here soon, Daddy." Chelsea happily munched her nachos, scooping up salsa with tortilla chips.

From all the multitude of sautéed, boiled, baked, fried food, she chose this simple fare that actually came free with the meal. But as long as she was happy.

Despite hunger pangs, he decided to wait to order for himself until Kristina arrived. Tapping against the tile increased.

Worry tightened his gut. Hopefully, this restaurant didn't serve any seafood. Surely, there was none in Chelsea's nachos, but what about cross-contamination? As he'd decided, he'd called the restaurant in advance to tell them about Chelsea's shellfish allergy and he'd remind the server, too.

His poor girl! As much as he loved indulging her, eating out with Chelsea was difficult. He couldn't wait until the house was ready to move in and he'd start cooking for her again.

Maybe he'd even cook a meal and invite Roman and Kristina.

Whoa.

Where had that thought come from? Warmth rose inside him.

He ruffled Chelsea's hair, her blonde curls soft under his fingertips, and breathed in the sweet mango-shampoo scent. In his mind, he went over the list of things Roman said they had in Chapel Cove.

"Would you like to go to the park later?" As some salsa got smeared on Chelsea's face, he carefully wiped the corner of his daughter's mouth with a napkin.

The child clapped. "Yes, Daddy! Can we take Miss Kristina? I miss her."

A longing in his heart told him he missed her, too, though he didn't want to admit it. He looked forward to spending a day with Kristina and Chelsea.

Stop.

The napkin slid out of his hand and whooshed onto the table.

When was the last time he'd eagerly expected a new day? That was right—back when Sally had been still alive. For two years, he mostly tried to survive the next day, doing his best to keep his child happy.

A whoosh of movement at his left alerted him as his daughter abandoned her nachos and darted to the entrance.

"Chelsea!" He ran after her, weaving between patrons. But he nearly tripped when he saw the person his daughter was running to.

In a shimmering daffodil-colored dress and canary-hued jacket, Kristina was like sunshine. Her hair, swept up in an elegant hairdo, caught the soft overhead lights, reflecting a myriad of minuscule sparkles. And some kind of lemon-colored flower decorated it. High-heeled shoes matched the flower while subtle rouge highlighted her high cheekbones and eyeshadow accentuated her brown eyes.

He could live without wine-hued lipstick on her lips because it made him think of kissing her, and his intoxicated heartbeat increased. So not the thoughts he should be having.

In an inexplicable way, she was glowing as she stopped to catch Chelsea. He was so taken away with Kristina that it took a lot of willpower to look away and watch after his daughter.

A soft smile touched those bright, slightly plump lips as Kristina bent and hugged Chelsea. "I'm happy to see you, too."

At that moment, he knew his life was about to change.

He didn't know yet how or when, but he was certain. A ray of sunshine reached something deep inside him, something he thought died with Sally, and long-dormant hope was waking up to life again.

Sally's words about a new love in his life appeared in his mind. But of course, she couldn't have foreseen this. It was merely a coincidence.

As he finished the short distance to his date—no, dinner partner—he realized he wasn't the only one staring. Nearly every male patron was watching her.

"Hello, Kristina. You look beautiful." He struggled for words. Beautiful? No. So much more—radiant, lovely, amazing! Somehow, those words didn't roll off his tongue.

"You're just being nice, but thank you." She straightened out and placed her hand on Chelsea's shoulder.

Kristina and his daughter were so different, and at the same time, they looked as if they belonged together.

No, thinking that way was ridiculous. As he walked them to the table, he did his best to rein in his runaway thoughts. After the way he'd felt toward Sally, nobody could replace her. And Kristina's brother said she wasn't looking for a romantic relationship. But instead of comforting him, that statement left him soured.

Did he like her?

As he pulled a chair for her and savored the tantalizing scent of her flowery perfume, he knew the answer. But it was becoming much more than *like* if he started thinking whether Kristina would make a good mom for Chelsea.

Lord, please help me. Please guide me here. It has to be all about my daughter now. Why am I feeling this way then?

Turning to the Lord again was easier than he'd thought. But he couldn't forget how much he'd prayed in the hospital, and still, Sally died.

As they all sat down, his and Kristina's gazes met and held, and he couldn't tear his from her. It became difficult to breathe.

Then his gaze slipped to her luscious lips again, and he wanted to taste them much more than the restaurant fare.

Get a grip.

He moved his gaze to her eyes, but as they widened and longing appeared, his palms sweat. The attraction between them was so tangible he felt he could touch it. He handed her the sunrise-colored rose.

An adorable blush brightened her suntanned face as she breathed in the aroma. "You shouldn't have. This is not a date."

"If it was a date, you'd have a few dozen red roses. Besides, Chelsea chose it. You're not going to refuse her gift, are you?" Okay, maybe he wasn't playing fair.

His daughter stuck out her lower lip. "You don't like it?"

Kristina placed the flower aside as she smiled at his child. "I love it."

He could look at her forever....

"What would you like to drink?" The waitress's voice pulled him out of his daze.

He waved to Kristina, letting her go first.

"Iced tea." She leaned to Chelsea. "What about you, sweetie?"

Her attention to his daughter tugged at his chest.

"Me, too." Then his little girl pushed the chip bowl toward Kristina. "Wanna some nachos?"

"Thank you. Sure, as soon as we say grace." She brushed a strand of hair aside from Chelsea's face. Then she looked up at the waitress. "I already know what I want to order. Beef tamales, please."

"Me, too!" Chelsea grinned at her.

Huh. Well, he studied the restaurant menu enough before coming here to know there couldn't be shellfish in them. "I'll take *caldo de res*. Please make sure no seafood comes anywhere close to my daughter's order. She's allergic to shellfish." He opted for the iced tea, as well.

The waitress, a young girl with green streaks in her hair and a matching lipstick, probably still in high school, wrote down the order, nodded, and left.

Kristina took Chelsea's hand, and Greg circled his around her fragile fingers before enveloping his daughter's tiny palm. They all bowed their heads.

"Dear Heavenly Father, thank You for this food we're about to eat and please bless it," Kristina whispered. "Please help Greg and Chelsea and make them happy. And please help my daughters, Leanna and Reanna, and for Leanna to speak to me again. Also, please help my brother. In Jesus's holy name, amen."

Touched she included him and Chelsea in her prayers, he opened his eyes, and something shifted inside him even as his gut twisted. Kristina's daughter wasn't speaking to her? Could he help in some way? And what if the day came when Chelsea distanced herself from him?

He'd have to let her go eventually, sure, but not to that degree.

This nearly felt like a family dinner. Something pleasant uncoiled in the pit of his stomach. Could he ever hope for a family again? Just a few days ago, he wouldn't think that way. It didn't make sense to think that way now, especially with a divorcee who'd given up on men.

The young waitress brought their drinks, and he sipped cold, sweet, refreshing liquid.

"I'm sorry about Leanna," he said quietly as Chelsea returned to her nachos, this time pretending she was sharing them with Taco.

Pain flashed in Kristina's eyes. "She's just hurt Cullen and I divorced. But I miss her so much. I miss both of my girls." She sent a tender glance toward his daughter. "Enjoy every moment. They do grow up fast."

"I know." Bending down, he placed a kiss atop his little girl's head, getting a whiff of mango shampoo again. Tenderness expanded his chest. "Every moment is precious."

The crunching sound got louder. Chelsea was really making a dent in those nachos.

He moved back. "Sweetheart, wait until the main meal."

He probably should've kept the tortilla chips away from her, in order not to ruin her appetite. He still tried to figure out this parenting stuff, and he kept making mistakes. And he *was* spoiling her rotten.

"You're doing great with her." Kristina seemed to read his doubts.

Her reassurance warmed his neck. But he needed to correct the thing he didn't do so great. "Could you take over the repairs on the house, please? I mean, if you still would like to do it."

"I'll be happy to." Her expression didn't show any surprise as she swirled her tea. Her brother probably already told her.

Unless… No, Kristina wouldn't do that.

"Yeah!" An enthusiastic nod made Chelsea's bangs jump up and down. "I wanna my room with purple elephants. And then Chip could live with us. And we could eat breakfast at home."

"I thought you liked it when I cooked for you at Grandpa and Grandma's."

His daughter looked down. "Yeah. But you're always upset after you talk to them."

He swallowed, lost for words. His daughter was attentive beyond her age.

"I'll be happy to take over repairs," Kristina hurried to add. She drew something with her finger on the table. "I love doing repairs. But it's probably too late to start a new career at forty."

Deep sadness in her voice made him cringe, and he had a strong urge to take her hand. Purely to show his support, of course. "It's never too late to start doing what you love. Some people do it when they are eighty. You're actually forty years ahead."

She chuckled. "I'm not even sure what exactly I want to do. Cullen insisted I took care of the girls and the house. Apart from his calling me useless sometimes, I was happy being a stay-at-home mom. But the twins don't need me anymore."

That Cullen guy sounded more and more like a jerk. "Was there something you did when you were a kid that still makes your heart sing?"

"Interior design." Her face brightened, but then concern shadowed her lovely eyes. "But I don't have a degree. I don't have a portfolio. Besides some pro bono work in repairs, zero experience working with clients." She took another sip. "Who is going to hire me?"

"I would." *Right, buddy. Sure, you would.* He'd given the job to her brother first. And then took it away from him, which wasn't fair to Roman. "Don't get me wrong. Your brother did a great job. Um, I'd love to invite both of you to a picnic at the park."

"Yeah! A picnic!" Chelsea waved with her nacho.

"What?" Kristina's eyes widened, and she started coughing.

Was she going to choke? He shot up from his chair, but her cough already quieted.

"I don't think my brother will be able to come." She blinked fast as tears, probably from coughing, appeared in her eyes.

He quirked an eyebrow. "You don't know what time and day I had in mind."

"He is, um, busy." She looked away.

Uh-oh. Roman probably wasn't too happy with him. Greg's frown deepened. He really wanted Roman to become a friend. As for Kristina…

Let's face it, he wanted to be more than friends with her.

So not a good idea.

The click of heels against the tile and the mouthwatering scent of beef soup announced the young waitress's return. Would Chelsea want to do the same emerald-hued streaks in her hair when she became a teenager?

"Leanna colored her hair purple when she turned fifteen," Kristina whispered to him.

Huh. How could they be so in accord after knowing each other for so little time? He could really use some of her expertise in parenting. And the aura of softness, kindness, and hard-earned wisdom around her made spending time in her company especially pleasant.

His rib cage constricted. Yes, he was attracted to her, but his heart had already been given away. Once and forever.

He unwrapped tamales for Chelsea and cut them with a fork. Then he took a few spoonfuls of his flavorful soup while they ate in companionable silence.

Then his daughter's fork clattered to the plate. "Daddy, I don't feel so good."

Alarm shot through him. "What's wrong, honey?"

Concern in her eyes, Kristina leaned to his daughter. "Sweetie? Where does it hurt?"

His girl turned pale. She wrapped her small arms around her stomach. "Tummy hurts."

He leaped to his feet, and so did Kristina.

His child started wheezing, and his heart dropped to the floor. "No! She might be having an allergic reaction to shellfish."

Beef tamales didn't contain any seafood, but there was probably cross-contamination in the kitchen. Had he missed a seafood item in the menu? What was he thinking bringing his child to the restaurant?

He lifted his trembling daughter from the chair as everything inside him quaked, as well. "I need you to lie down, okay? You're going to feel better soon." At least, he hoped so.

Kristina fished out her cell phone. "You have EpiPen with you, right? I'll call 911."

Thankfully, he always had an autoinjector with him. The danger of his daughter having an anaphylactic shock and possibly dying filled his every cell with terror. "Call the clinic. I'll do the EpiPen injection. Then we'll take Chelsea to see the clinic doctor in case there's a secondary reaction."

It was getting late, but even in a small town, they should have a doctor on call.

Chelsea's blue eyes grew big as she pointed to her throat. She couldn't speak! She was obviously scared. So was he.

Lord, please help my little girl. Please!

CHAPTER EIGHT

AS A crowd started gathering around them, Greg gestured for them to hold back. "Please give us space."

Kristina put her phone on the speakerphone and placed it on the table. While listening to long beeps, she shrugged out of her jacket and threw it on the floor. "Let's put her there."

His hands shaking, he carefully lowered his daughter onto the soft fabric. Then he ripped off his own jacket and tucked it under Chelsea's head. Every second counted.

While Kristina talked to someone, he took the EpiPen out of his slacks pocket and removed the injector from its case.

"What's going on? What's happening?" people around them muttered.

He tuned out background voices as he leaned to his daughter, holding the injector in the middle. "Sweetheart, I'm going to do a little injection. It's going to be okay. Please stay still."

But the girl's eyes only grew bigger, and she wiggled.

If she moves away when I inject, the injection will be useless.

Cold sweat beaded on his forehead.

Kristina finished the call, disconnected, and dropped to her knees. "I'll hold her leg."

His heart thundering, he took off the blue safety cap and willed his hands to stop trembling. Whispering something soothing to Chelsea, Kristina held the girl's right leg still.

The previous time this happened, he'd been the one holding Chelsea, and Sally had administered help. He needed to remember all the movements precisely. He pressed the orange tip to the middle of his daughter's thigh.

A click told him the injection occurred. His pulse in high gear, he held the apparatus against the little thigh and counted in his mind, "One one thousand, two one thousand..."

When he reached "ten one thousand," he removed the EpiPen and rubbed the injection site. He had a backup EpiPen, but he really hoped he wouldn't need it.

Chelsea stopped wheezing.

"Daddy, scared." Her weak voice soothed his ears. She could speak again!

Applause around them erupted, but he didn't care for any cheering. He scooped his daughter up, so fragile in his arms. "See, you're already feeling better. But we'll go visit a nice doctor just to make sure."

"Daddy, Taco?" She lifted dewy eyes at him.

He closed his eyes and then opened them. His daughter nearly stopped breathing, and she worried about leaving a toy behind.

"I'll get Taco, sweetie." Kristina picked up both jackets and left a few bills on the table. Then she grabbed the elephant and tucked it in her purse. "I called the clinic. Dr. Jeff Johnson will wait for us there. He's great with kids. You're going to love him, sweetie."

Even in this turmoil, gratitude stirred inside him. "Thank you," he whispered to Kristina before rushing to the exit.

Based on the quick footfalls behind him, she kept up.

The air outside was slightly cooler now, so he wrapped his arms tighter around his child. "Are you okay?"

"Yes, Daddy." Her voice was tiny.

Well, at least she could talk. His heart hammering in his ears, he made it to his truck.

Still holding his child, he reached into his pocket for his keys. But his hand shook so badly, the keys clattered to the ground.

He took a lungful of cool, fresh air. He really needed to pull himself together. The worst was behind them. He hoped.

Kristina scooped up the car keys. "Let me drive, please. It's going to be better for Chelsea if you sit in the back with her. That way, you can calm her down, if needed. And monitor her breathing, in case a second injection is required."

At her gesture and the expression in her dark eyes, more gratitude blossomed in his chest. She even tried to protect his self-respect by coming up with an important reason to take over driving. She didn't mention she probably knew the way to the clinic better than he did.

"Good idea." He nodded.

She clicked the fob and opened the truck door.

"Thanks." He placed his daughter in the booster seat.

Her complexion was returning to normal, and her breathing becoming even. Air whooshed out of his lungs as he buckled her up. They weren't safe yet, but ice no longer filled his veins.

Kristina revved the motor. Warm air spread in the truck, so she obviously turned on the heat, too. "I'll get there as soon as I can." Then she twisted to hand Chelsea the toy elephant. "I'm sure Taco missed you."

"Hello, Taco." The corners of his daughter's mouth lifted up.

He slid near her. "I love you so much, sweetheart."

"Love you, too, Daddy."

He said a prayer of gratitude for Chelsea being able to breathe again.

The second prayer was to thank the Lord for Kristina being with him right now.

Kristina's fingers tightened around the steering wheel as she sped through Chapel Cove. Hopefully, Dr. Jeff Johnson would be waiting for them at the clinic.

Her heart racing, she glanced in the rearview mirror. Greg leaned over his daughter, his arm draped over her protectively. Something more than compassion stirred inside her. His love for his child was overwhelming.

She returned her attention to the road and made a turn. She'd been through some scary situations with her twins, but she'd always had to deal with them alone. Cullen had been busy at work or rather, as she realized now, having affairs. How could she have been so blind for many years? She'd probably been reluctant to admit her marriage was falling apart. Well, it had fallen apart, anyway.

No matter. Not her past heartache, but Chelsea's present was important now. But the difference between Cullen and Greg was so evident it endeared him to her even more.

No thinking like that!

She pulled up to the clinic's entrance. "I'll drop you off here and then go park."

"Okay. Thank you." His voice was stronger now.

After he left with Chelsea and the door slammed closed, she glided into the nearest vacant spot. She picked up his jacket from the seat, still fresh with his expensive cologne, and her heart made a strange movement.

She was developing feelings for him. Strong feelings.

No time to think about it now.

After a mad dash to the entrance, she entered the stucco building.

Seascapes, hanging on white walls with molding the color of yesterday's coffee, depicted what could be the Oregon coast on a tranquil spring day while an indigo ceramic vase on a dark alder coffee table shadowed a colorful stack of magazines. Greg slumped in a faux-leather chair matching the vase, his daughter on his lap.

The girl still looked pale, and worry tightened its grasp around Kristina's heart.

He sent a grateful and a tad guilty smile her way. "I'm sorry for the way dinner turned out."

"If Chelsea is okay, it turned out great to me." Wishing her hometown had a pediatrician, she approached his chair.

As much as she loved visiting Dr. Johnson as a kid, he was getting old and close to retirement, and Chapel Cove was growing, with more children born. It would be nice to have some toys and children's books when Chelsea and other kids had to visit a doctor.

"I do appreciate all you've done," Greg said as she got close.

The door to her right opened, and a nurse in butter-hued scrubs stepped out, interrupting any lucid response she would have given. "Dr. Johnson will see you now."

Kristina exhaled her relief. So both the doctor and the nurse had made it here already. She stepped toward the door but forced herself to stop.

Cradling his child, Greg got up. "You're welcome to come with us." He walked to the door.

She hesitated, then shook her head. She wasn't part of this small family, and she'd best not harbor any illusions. "I'll wait here."

Chelsea handed her the toy. "Taco will stay with you so you're not alone."

Oh, precious, precious child. Tears prickled behind Kristina's eyes as she took the elephant from the girl's tiny hands. "Yes. Thank you. He'll keep me company."

Who was she kidding? Not harbor any illusions? She was attached far too much already.

She sank onto the chair and slipped the toy into her purse. But only a few seconds later, she jumped and started pacing the large gray tile.

Her phone rang. She stilled and fished it from her purse. Nai.

Kristina swiped the screen to answer. "Hello, Nai."

"Hello, *amiga*. I heard what happened at the restaurant. Are you all right?" Concern tightened her friend's voice.

Kristina plunked herself in a chair again. News did travel fast in small towns. But her shoulders relaxed as her grip loosened around the phone as if holding onto her dear friend's hand. *Thank You, God, for Nai.* "I'm not the one who nearly went into anaphylactic shock."

"You know what I mean."

"Chelsea is doing better. She's with the doctor right now." Kristina breathed in the now-familiar woodsy scent coming from Greg's jacket and went slightly dizzy. In moments like this, imagining him drawing her close, lowering his head, and claiming her lips with his was completely inappropriate. Her pulse spiked. "I keep imagining him kissing me. I can't stop thinking about him. I'm falling for him."

"Don't say it in such a tragic voice." Teasing notes danced in Nai's voice. "It might be a good thing."

Kristina groaned. "He's a grieving widower. And I'm burned on men. And Greg is way younger than I am, to top it off!"

"Yeah. Of all men in Chapel Cove, you had to choose a handsome, muscular, well-off young guy who apparently also has a kind heart. I mean, really, what do you see in him?"

Where was that quiet friend who never would've teased like this? Kristina managed to suppress the second groan. "You're not helping. And then that thing with me being Roman. No, impersonating Roman. Well, you know."

"I know." Nai lowered her voice. "So, what are you going to do? Stop seeing Greg?"

"Impossible. He just offered me the job to take over his repairs."

Her friend's chuckle traveled down the line. "See, you won't have to wear a mustache and beard any longer. Things are already looking up."

"Nai!" The door opened. Kristina whispered into the phone, "Gotta go. We'll talk later, okay?"

"Yep, and I'll want to hear all about that kiss." Laughing, Nai disconnected.

Kristina didn't have time to cringe. She hurried to Greg and his child, whose head was resting on his shoulder. Chelsea's eyes were closed, and she seemed to drift off asleep. She must be exhausted. And antihistamines Dr. Johnson had probably given her could make her sleepy. She remembered that from the scary episode with her twins' allergic reaction to eggs and a subsequent visit to the ER. She shuddered. She'd been scared to death then, so she could easily relate to what Greg had gone through tonight.

"How is she?" she whispered as she met them halfway.

Tiredness settled in his handsome features, but his blue eyes shone brighter. "The doctor gave her IV steroids and antihistamines. He was going to give a prescription for a new EpiPen, but he said the pharmacy was closed by now. So he gave us an extra injector and a supply of pills," he said in a low voice, probably so as not wake up the child.

"How kind of Dr. Johnson." She kept her voice low, as well.

Well, the doctor probably charged for it, but still getting medicine in time helped a lot.

Greg lowered himself in the seat with caution, as if doing his best not to disturb Chelsea. "He examined her and had the nurse take her vital signs. Chelsea seems fine. Still, he wants to keep her here for a couple of hours for observation."

"Makes sense." A wave of tenderness swept her up as she sat down near him and studied the sleeping girl. Though she looked nothing like Leanna and Reanna, she still reminded Kristina of the twins when they were little.

And then his hand found hers, and a different wave swept Kristina up as she leaned toward him. A wave of attraction. She made the mistake of looking into his eyes and lost herself there.

Yes, she was falling for a man whose heart was closed to romantic feelings, and she had no clue what to do about it. If she stayed near him a moment longer, she'd forget everything and kiss him.

She eased her hand out of his, placed his jacket near him, and jumped to her feet. "You must be starved. How about I'll get hamburgers from a drive-through?"

"Very considerate of you. But at least let me pay for the meal. I owe you too much as it is."

"No. Don't disturb Chelsea." She rushed outside as fast as she could. She'd get something for Chelsea, as well. She'd ask Roman for help.

But as she drove back with hamburgers in a paper bag, an enticing scent making her stomach growl, a longing to see Greg soon told her she couldn't run away from herself or her budding feelings for him.

No matter how much she tried.

His face lit up when she entered the empty clinic, and that in turn lit up something inside her.

She sat down beside him, bowed her head, and said grace.

And then once again, she added a prayer of gratitude over Chelsea feeling better.

"Thank you for doing this." Gratitude settled in Greg's eyes.

"Happy to. I also called Roman on the way, and he made a loaded pastrami sandwich for when Chelsea would wake up. I explained about her shellfish allergy, and he assured me no seafood came anywhere close to the sandwich. I picked it up on the way here and made sure to keep it separate from the drive-through food, just in case." When she bit into her hamburger, juicy meat exploded over her tongue, crisp lettuce adding bite to one of the best things she'd ever eaten.

"You're amazing." Greg moved his hand carefully as he ate, as if not to wake up his daughter.

Keeping their voices low, they chatted about their favorite movies, singers, sports, and found they had similar tastes in many things. He told her about his time as a snowboarder and the thrill of flying on the slopes, and she shared her bucket list, written at thirteen, which included something crazy, maybe snowboarding from a mountain.

Uh-oh. "Not that I think you're crazy." Better return to safer topics. Music, for example. She munched on the fry. "I'm surprised you like classical music, though." As her hand wrapped around a smooth, cold plastic cup, she flushed down the food with the iced tea.

His hand with the hamburger froze. "Sally dragged me to a classical music concert. I tried to talk my way out of it before finally giving up, but after a few minutes there, I started enjoying it." He put the hamburger aside.

Leaning forward, she listened, drawn to him so much she wanted to know everything about him. Including his love for a different woman. Yes, she truly must be a sucker for punishment.

A faraway look glazed those blue eyes. "I'll always remember the first time I met Sally. It was at a Colorado ski resort. She wasn't great at sports, but her friends talked her into going. She was dressed in a powder blue suit that matched her eyes, and her cheeks were rosy from frost." He paused as if lost in those times.

Kristina kept silent.

Then he continued, "The moment she put on skis, she fell. She tried again and fell again. Instead of getting grouchy, she laughed. I don't know why, but the instant I saw her, I knew she was the one for me. I worked as a ski instructor there at the time while improving my snowboarding skills. I taught her to ski, and she taught me everything else. If it's okay to ask, was it love at first sight for you and Cullen, too?"

She snorted as she downed her iced tea. Her story wasn't nearly as romantic. "Quite the opposite. I worked as a waitress at Tía Irma's to help my family make ends meet. Cullen was in Chapel Cove for a vacation at the beach. In the spring of my senior year, he walked into the restaurant in an expensive suit and with a golden watch, behaving as if he owned the place and expected to be served before other customers. I made him wait his turn. Surprisingly, that made him pay more attention to me. When he started giving me compliments, I cut him off. I was polite but cold. He left a huge tip."

Greg didn't say a word, just kept looking at her as if her story were important to him.

She munched on a fry. "The next day, he came again—with much less arrogance. When he asked me out, I told him I didn't see any point dating a vacationer. He kept coming and inviting me a few more days. Then he disappeared, and I figured he went back to Portland and forgot about him."

Would she have been better off if he'd never come back? But even bad things happened for a reason, and she'd learned a lot from her marriage, for example, how to be patient, tactful, and grateful for the kindness of others since she'd received little kindness at home. And of course, she had two wonderful daughters, even if one of them refused to speak to her now.

"What happened next?" Greg's quiet voice interrupted her thoughts.

"Oh yes. In the summer, he came back with expensive presents for my mother and me. Eventually, I figured going out with him and sending him on his merry way was easier than refusing his advances. He took me to see two amazing gardens and waterfalls in Portland and then to a candlelit dinner."

She dipped another fry into ketchup but didn't bring it to her mouth as her throat constricted. She'd held onto those beautiful memories the first few years of marriage—until the infidelities started and the memories began feeling as false as his promises of undying love.

"For days, he showered me with flowers, gifts, and compliments. He knew a lot about different cuisines, movies, cities, you name it. He was older than I was but had handsome features and gray eyes I started getting attracted to. Whatever I wanted, he threw to my feet. I felt admired and needed and started finding his company pleasant." She paused and pushed a few fries past the lump in her throat.

How could one man act so differently?

"He gave me a car as a graduation present. I didn't want to take it, but he insisted. He said if I married him, he'd pay for my degree in interior design, help my brother set up his business, buy a restaurant for my mother. For our honeymoon, we'd go to India." She sighed.

"But you never did." The words weren't a question but a statement, and compassion flashed in Greg's eyes.

"Maybe I deserve what happened after several years of marriage because I probably fell in love more with his promise to make my dreams come true than with the man himself." She chased down bitter thoughts with sweet tea.

"Nobody deserves bad treatment." Greg touched her hand. "And it wasn't right of him to deceive you. Because something tells me his promises never materialized."

She looked at sleeping Chelsea with the same gentleness she'd felt toward her daughters. "For our honeymoon, we drove to Las Vegas. He took me to some great shows, but I didn't gamble, so I stayed in the hotel room when he did. When we returned, there were always excuses for why things had to be postponed. Then I gave birth to twins. I got pregnant on our honeymoon. Cullen got colder and colder and criticized me instead of giving compliments."

A muscle in Greg's jaw twitched. "He sounds like a horrible husband."

She snorted and took a bite of her juicy hamburger. No reason for Cullen to spoil her meal like he'd ruined many during their marriage. "According to him, he was a great husband. He took me out of poverty, so I should appreciate the rich life he was giving me instead of nagging about college. I should appreciate the chance to spend more time with my babies instead of putting them in daycare. There would be time to travel to India or get a degree later. How could I be so selfish? He could've married a much more beautiful, sophisticated woman like his friends did."

"That's ridiculous." Indignation flashed in his eyes. "Oh. I didn't mean to interrupt."

"I didn't know how to dress, wasn't into recent gossip, and rarely cooked a meal well enough to please him. I tried so hard to make him happy. But I always was too short, too clumsy, too fat, too plain—well, you get the idea." She sipped her *iced* tea, the way her marriage turned out to be.

"Why didn't you leave?"

She bit into her hamburger again and chewed on the juicy meat and just the right amount of lettuce, tomatoes, and pickles. "More than once, I wanted to leave. But I gave my vow, and I wanted the twins to have a father. So I dedicated my life to my daughters while doing my best to revive the passion he'd once felt for me. Or at least I hoped he did because he referred to me as the most difficult case he'd ever won."

Greg's jaw set in a stubborn line. "I'd love to tell him a few kind words."

Maybe it was better to change the topic. She hushed Cullen's diminishing words in her head. "You said you don't know yet what you want to do in Chapel Cove. What were you ever passionate about?"

His eyes lit up. "Snowboarding. But raising Chelsea is more important."

She sipped her iced tea. "What about selling sports equipment? Did you enjoy doing it in Portland?"

"Hmmm. I did. I liked talking to customers, giving them pointers. But is Chapel Cove big enough to support such a store?"

She started counting on her fingers. "We've got hiking, windsurfing, parasailing, bicycling…"

He smiled. "Then, I guess, there's only one way to find out."

His little girl stirred, and Kristina pressed a finger to her mouth. They finished their meal in silence. She didn't have to count calories anymore, afraid Cullen would ridicule her for extra pounds again.

Greg's words about her looking beautiful warmed her inside. But Cullen had been generous with compliments before marriage, too. Would Greg change as drastically if she surrendered her heart?

CHAPTER NINE

WHEN, two hours later, Greg pulled up to the Tía Irma's parking lot, Kristina glanced back at the sleeping child, and tenderness filled her. A soft smile played on the girl's lips.

Greg turned off the engine and glanced back, as well. Concern dissipated from his eyes. "It's difficult to believe that, only a few hours ago, she gave us such a huge scare. I'm sorry you went through this, but I'm glad you were here with me, with us."

"I'm glad I was with you, too." She meant it. She placed her hand on the cold metallic handle as something shifted in her chest.

She didn't want to leave. And not only because she worried about the little girl. She was drawn to this man beyond comprehension.

"Hold on." He left the truck, rushed around, and opened the door for her.

As a wave of cold air met her, she moved her legs carefully, hopefully ladylike, but she knew her feet wouldn't reach the ground from the tall truck.

As if realizing her dilemma, he fit his hands around her waist and lifted her. By the time he set her on the ground, her heart jumped into her throat, and her breathing couldn't be shallower.

He took off his jacket and put it around her shoulders, giving her warmth and a whiff of expensive cologne. "Have I told you how beautiful you look tonight?" He tucked a strand of hair behind her ear.

Okay, she was wrong. Her breathing could go shallower. It just did. "Right. Beautiful. My eyelids are drooping, and my makeup is probably smudged."

His eyes darkened. "You're a very attractive woman. Why do you diminish yourself so much?"

Must be all those years married to Cullen. She straightened her spine to its full capacity. "I guess I wasn't spoiled by male attention."

"That's a shame." He threw a quick glance at the window as if to confirm his daughter was still sleeping and leaned to Kristina. "It's about time it's corrected." He traced the outline of her face with his fingertips.

Every cell in her body woke up to life. Who'd think that at the age of forty she'd feel more like a woman than in her twenties? Savoring unfamiliar sensations, she rose on her toes.

Even Cullen hadn't made her feel this way, and she'd loved him—she really had. A sting of guilt made her close her eyes, but when she opened them, she was closer to Greg as if drawn by a strong magnet. What was happening to her?

"I want you to feel treasured." Staring in her eyes, he cupped her face. "Admired." His gaze slid to her lips. "Cherished."

He was going to kiss her.

Wasn't he?

Please kiss me.

Sweet anticipation spreading through her, she slid her arms around his neck. She started feeling all those things when she was with him. Treasured, admired, cherished. But he didn't say *loved.*

And that's what she wanted so badly.

Love me.

She stilled for a moment, but then he brought her nearer. His emotion-darkened eyes peering into hers, he dipped his head. She went deliciously dizzy just waiting for his lips to brush against hers.

"Daddy!" Chelsea's sleepy voice drifted from the truck.

Kristina didn't know who eased back first, but when she looked up into his eyes, their expression changed to concern.

He moved away. "Yes, sweetheart."

The cold night air seeped all the way to Kristina's heart. She shrugged out of his jacket and handed it to him. Then she took out the toy from her purse and gave it over as well. "Good-bye, Greg. Give Chelsea Taco back, please, and tell her good-bye for me."

His skin brushed against hers as he accepted the elephant. "Kristina, wait."

"It's late." She whirled around and sprinted to her car, scuffling awkwardly on high heels. She resisted the urge to take her shoes off and run barefoot. With her propensity to trip over everything, the last thing she needed was to drop to the ground right now.

There was no reason to feel this disappointment. But was it too late for her, too? To hope there could be something between her and Greg?

He was a single father and a widower, still hurting from his loss. And she was a recent divorcee. She shouldn't let herself fall for him.

As she clicked her car fob, heavy footfalls behind her made her turn around.

Greg touched her forearm, sending tingles along her skin. "Chelsea says she and Taco want to see you tomorrow."

She couldn't help smiling. "Chelsea and Taco, huh?"

He returned her smile. "Well, me, too. We *all* want to see you tomorrow."

"I'll think about that. Give Chelsea a kiss for me. Like that." She lifted herself on her toes and placed a kiss on his cheek, his five-o'clock shadow slightly rough against her lips. A pleasant wave spread through her.

Laughter and something else erupted in his eyes. "I think she'd like to kiss you back."

Kristina's heart leaped into her throat again. She really needed to control her emotions better. "No. I've got to go, and you've got to go, too."

"Right." He opened her car door for her.

As she slipped into the driver's seat of her old sedan, her heart was beating fast. No, she shouldn't let herself fall for him.

But it looked too late for that, too.

The next morning, eyes half-opened, Kristina pressed the button to dismiss her cell phone alarm. The alarm continued ringing. Suppressing a groan, she opened her eyes with an effort. She was getting too old for going to bed late and getting up early.

Oh.

There was a reason the alarm refused to get quiet. It wasn't the alarm ringing, but Greg calling. And she overslept again.

Seriously?

Nine a.m. already, and she was supposed to be at his house by eight a.m.

This time, a groan did escape. Her first day on the job—well, her first day on the job as *herself*—and she was late.

Great!

She sat up fast and swiped the screen. "Greg, I'm so sorry. I guess I somehow dismissed the alarm in my sleep and didn't notice it. I'll be there as soon as I can." Not having to put on a man's disguise should help her get ready quicker, but he didn't need to know such details.

"Don't worry about it. You spent half of the night in the clinic, so I really should ask you to start tomorrow."

"No!" Did she say it too soon? And of course, she protested because he and Chelsea needed to move into the house, not because she wanted to see him—badly. Keeping the phone near her ear, she rushed to the bathroom. And nearly tripped over sleeping Chip.

"Sorry, Chip." She scooted around him.

The puppy yawned and settled back to sleep. Judging by the gnawed table legs, he'd had a full night's work and needed rest.

She sighed as she opened the toothpaste. "I'll be there soon. Honest."

"I'm going to spend the day with my daughter. After yesterday... You understand, right?" His voice dipped. "The key is under the doormat."

Her hand with the toothbrush froze in the air. "Of course, I understand. Totally." She even managed to sound upbeat. Absolutely no reason for the disappointment sluicing through her. "I'll see you... when I see you."

"Wait. Don't you need me to tell you what needs to be done?"

Huh. "Um. My brother already told me." She disconnected and brushed her teeth furiously. The emptiness inside made it clear she missed Greg already.

Ridiculous.

She rinsed her teeth, wiped her face with a soft towel, and headed back to her bedroom to take care of the cute dachshund. She was a grown-up woman with two grown-up daughters. Not some love-struck teenager. She'd get over this silly attraction.

"Right, Chip?" She snuggled the puppy and carried him to the kitchen.

Chip barked something that could be construed as an agreement.

After feeding him and taking him outside to do his business, she decided to spare Roman from dog-sitting as she pulled on her worn-out jeans and an old sweater.

"Behave. You have toys to chew on." She wiggled her finger at the puppy but had a strong feeling she'd have more chewed furniture when she got home.

As if apologizing, Chip licked her hand.

She patted his short smooth fur. "At least don't shred it into pieces."

The way her heart was probably going to be.

Greg glanced at the dashboard as he drove up to his house. Four p.m. Spending most of the day at the park with Chelsea was fun, but in the end the two of them—and according to his daughter, Taco—agreed that they missed Kristina.

He turned off the engine and twisted back. "Do you think she'll like the surprise?" Hmmm. Or would she be disappointed having her work interrupted?

"Yeah!" His little girl grinned.

He'd never get tired of seeing that sweet smile. Who'd think that only yesterday…

No, best not to reminisce about it.

His phone rang. He fished it out of his jeans back pocket and grimaced. His former in-laws.

His relationship with Mr. and Mrs. Ronfrey was going from bad to worse, no matter how much he did his best to fix it. He even tried to pray for them because that's what Sally would do.

The prayer hadn't come easily.

He swiped his phone to answer. "Hello."

"We know everything." Mrs. Ronfrey's words seethed into his ear. "Our precious little girl nearly died yesterday! All because you had to entertain that Kristina woman by taking her to a restaurant. Have you forgotten Chelsea is allergic to shellfish? Or you simply didn't care at all!"

Though anger surged through his veins, he forced a smile as he turned to Chelsea. He covered the phone with his hand. "Just a moment, sweetheart. This is your grandma."

"Grandma!" She grinned and lifted her hands. "I wanna talk to Grandma."

His daughter's well-being was more important than his hurts. He had to remain calm for her sake. "Sure, sweetheart." Into the phone, he said, "Chelsea wants to talk to you. Thank God, she's perfectly fine. And Kristina actually helped us."

"Oh, really?"

"Here's your grandma," he said loud enough for Mrs. Ronfrey to hear and passed the phone to Chelsea.

While she chatted about something, he climbed out of his driver's seat and unbuckled her booster seat.

"I gonna see Miss Kristina. Bye, Grandma." His daughter handed him the phone.

He kept the smile firmly in place for her. "Good-bye, Mrs. Ronfrey," he said into the phone, making sure to sound even.

"Hold on." Eerie calm shivered through. "If that Kristina is more important to you than your own daughter, go ahead. We'll file for custody. Full custody."

Breathing became difficult. "You can't do that."

"Watch us. We'll find the way to declare you an unfit father." Then she disconnected.

The phone slid to the ground.

"Daddy?" His girl's voice filtered through his mental fog.

Could they really do that? No, it didn't make sense.

"Sorry, sweetheart." Keeping his voice calm took an effort, but he managed.

He picked up his phone and put it in the back pocket of his jeans. Then he removed Chelsea from the booster seat, placed her on the ground, and walked to the front door, her tiny palm drowned in his large hand.

He couldn't imagine losing Chelsea.

No, this had to be an empty threat.

His stomach tightened.

Wasn't it?

CHAPTER TEN

THE DOOR flung open before Greg had a chance to knock. Kristina had probably heard the motor's growl.

The way her eyes lit up was priceless. Clearly, she was glad to see them, and a pleasant wave rippling inside him promised he was thrilled to see her. The softness in her brown eyes soothed pain left over from his phone conversation.

As the lovely lips lifted, Kristina waved for them to enter.

"Hello, Miss Kristina!" Chelsea's hand slipped out of his, and she ran inside, then hugged Kristina's legs.

He closed the door behind him, wishing he could behave like a child and hug Kristina with the same enthusiasm. His blood rushed faster in his veins as he recalled having her in his arms yesterday. He'd nearly kissed her. And how badly he wanted to do it now!

Mrs. Ronfrey's words about filing for custody reverberated through his head, and a chill traveled down his spine. From what he knew about his former mother-in-law, she was capable of it.

"Hello, sweetie. Careful, I'm covered in paint." Kristina squatted and embraced his child. Then she released Chelsea, straightened out, and blinked up at him.

Uncertainty and longing in her doe-like eyes tugged at him, and he took a step toward her. He wanted to tell her so many things...

"Wow!" His daughter ran forward.

Uh-oh.

"Not so fast." He caught her midflight and put her on his shoulders, locking her in place. The last thing he wanted was for her to trip over something or land in a paint bucket.

"Let's go to my room!" She pointed forward.

"Let's do it." He marched to Chelsea's room.

As he walked through the house, he had to agree with her.

Wow.

The house was different already. The walls were brighter, and the rooms lighter, with smooth grays and arctic blues instead of their previous nearly black. Not to mention, the floors were so much cleaner. Kristina might've had a late start, but she'd done a lot in his absence.

Her soft footfalls followed them.

"Great job," he threw the words over his shoulder.

She touched his hand, and he felt it all the way to his heart. He felt things he shouldn't be feeling, especially after *the* conversation he'd had minutes ago. Since the moment Chelsea was born, he'd put her first. So he shouldn't be thinking about kissing Kristina right now.

Or ever.

Once he entered her room, Chelsea's squeal threw all other thoughts from his head.

His daughter clapped. "Purple elephants! A family! Daddy, Miss Kristina, and Chelsea." She pointed at one of the walls.

Ugh. He hoped Kristina wasn't offended being called an elephant. Bad enough that Cullen guy had persuaded her she was fat. Not that there was anything wrong with having curves.

"You're much slimmer than that," he whispered to her. Okay, that sounded awkward.

She chuckled. "I'm flattered to be called something Chelsea loves so much."

How easy Kristina was to talk to, how much fun to be around! Was it any wonder he was drawn to her? He stopped himself from moving closer. As their eyes met and held, his temperature rose.

Then she broke the eye contact as her gaze moved to his daughter. "Wait till you see the swing your dad and I... my..." She coughed a little. "My brother built together."

Your dad and I?

Suspicion crawled into his mind again, but he threw it away. Would Kristina try to impersonate her brother? No, that would be ridiculous.

"Yay!" For the second time, his baby squealed and clapped.

"Let me show you that swing." Joy filled his heart at seeing his precious girl so excited.

Being with Kristina not only made him happy. It made his daughter happy, too. He squelched hope inside him. There were too many obstacles to him and Kristina being together, and Mrs. Ronfrey just added a new one.

He carried Chelsea on his shoulders to the porch leading to the patio.

Whoa. Kristina had fixed the fence and the treacherous porch board.

"This is amazing. Thank you," he whispered to her as he strode to the swing hanging from the large maple tree. The air was cool, but dappled sunshine spilled through the budding branches. A few chickadees chirruped in the nearby aspens.

A smile lit up Kristina's pretty face. "My pleasure. This is going to be a great place."

"Yes. Thanks to you and your brother, it starts to feel like home." As he placed Chelsea on the swing and gave a push, he could see the renovated bathrooms and kitchen in his mind, could nearly smell the enticing scent of fajitas and pies.

And a certain petite Latina woman stood in front of his eyes, baking cookies with Chelsea, both of them laughing and making faces, and then the three of them decorating cookies. He'd probably have to get elephant shapes somewhere and purple sprinkles.

The image, the scents, and the sounds were so vivid he had to shake his head free of them.

On the other side of the swing, Kristina gave a little push, too.

Chelsea giggled. "Faster!"

He could easily make the swing fly fast, but he had to be careful. He didn't want his girl to fall.

His and Kristina's gazes met again. He shouldn't be losing himself in her dark eyes. But as he watched his daughter from the corner of his eye, a sense of simple delight he hadn't experienced in a long time entered him.

Maybe even wounds as deep as his could heal, couldn't they? With God, everything was possible. That's what Sally always said.

The thought about his late wife brought lingering sadness instead of the usual sharp pain.

Lord, please lead me on the path You want me to follow. I want to have the faith I once had. I just can't understand why Sally had to die.

After some time, Chelsea demanded, "Down. I wanna paint."

He suppressed a grimace as he brought the swing to a stop. "Sweetheart, not a good idea. You'll get dirty. Kristina and I can take care of painting."

The lower lip stuck out in a familiar expression. "Daddy, pretty-pretty please? I wanna help."

He might as well give up now and save them all some time. What were a ruined pink sweater and a stained pair of white pants compared to his child's smile? He could buy her a new outfit. He couldn't buy her happiness.

He raised a brow at Kristina. "Do we have a small brush?"

She nodded. "Sure thing. I'll bring a little bucket of outdoor paint for Chelsea to paint at the bottom of the patio door. How does that sound?"

"Sounds great."

At his agreement, she disappeared inside.

Outdoor paint, huh? She probably didn't want his daughter to breathe in the paint scents, and neither did he. Amazing that they were already this much in accord.

Soon Chelsea was humming some song as she dipped a tiny brush into paint and moved it along the bottom of the door, sticking the tip of her tongue out. He might as well make himself useful, but he didn't want to leave her. So he brought a can of outdoor paint and tools and started painting the wall nearby.

"I'll take care of the upper part of the patio doors." Kristina returned with the rest of the painting supplies.

"Tell me a story about Taco," Chelsea looked up at them.

He turned to Kristina, hoping she could come up with something because he certainly couldn't.

The brush froze in the air, and then Kristina continued moving it along the wall. "Well, let's see. Once upon a time..." She continued with a fun story about an elephant looking for breakfast and making friends on the way.

He could give her points for thinking fast.

When the tale ended, he nearly slapped himself on the forehead. "Chelsea and I ate, but I didn't even ask you if you had lunch—and it's time for dinner already." Judging by the work she'd done, she'd probably skipped her meal.

Kristina ducked her head. "I had a little something."

He had a feeling that "little something" didn't come close to a real meal.

"I owe you dinner. We'd love for you to join us." Now, he had a dilemma.

He couldn't take Chelsea to a restaurant again, and his former in-laws definitely wouldn't let him cook in their kitchen for Kristina. He should've rented a house instead of staying at the hotel.

"How about we finish here, and we all go to my rental? I'll make beef tacos." She lowered her voice. "There's no fish anywhere around my kitchen."

Great. Now he'd owe her two dinners. No, that wouldn't do. "I'll help cook." That's the least he could do.

"Me, too." Chelsea waved her paintbrush, sending drops of paint in all directions.

"Thanks. I could use some help." Kristina eyed the top spot of the door she couldn't reach. "Um, I'll go get a ladder."

"No need." He took her in his arms and lifted her up.

Big mistake. She did a sharp breath intake, and his heart started beating wildly. Having her in his arms wreaked havoc on his senses. Well, he wasn't one to retreat.

"Is this high enough?" His voice sounded husky to his own ears.

There was no answer. Wide-eyed, Kristina stared at him, her lips slightly parted. Okay, so this affected her as much as it affected him. At least his attraction wasn't one-sided. And thankfully, she didn't drop her paintbrush or a paint can on him.

The answer came from Chelsea. "A little higher, Daddy."

"Sure." His heart hammering, he lifted the petite beauty a few more inches.

Kristina finally seemed to find her voice. "That's good."

His muscles strained, but he could hold her in his arms forever.

His stomach tightened. With Sally's death, he'd learned there was no such thing as forever. What if things didn't work out and the breakup only added a new heartache into his daughter's life?

But what if they did? Was he ready for it? Would he ever be?

He made sure he watched his daughter as he held Kristina. But his thoughts were getting scrambled, and his heart beat faster and faster.

When a few minutes later she called out, "All done here," all questions disappeared from his head.

He let her slide in his arms until her eyes were level with his. Her breathing became uneven, and so did his. Her eyelashes fluttered, and her lips parted. For a few amazing moments, he just enjoyed having her close. Then he struggled against an overwhelming urge to taste her lips.

"Greg…" She tilted her head as if to make it easier for him.

No, his concentration should be on his daughter. He gathered whatever willpower he had left, which wasn't much.

With a sting of regret and guilt, he settled Kristina on the ground.

Disappointment flashed in her dark eyes, but then she bent toward Chelsea. "You're doing a fabulous job here, sweetie."

"Yeah?" The girl beamed up at her.

"Absolutely. Thank you so much for all your help. Let's just touch a little spot here." She took the brush from Chelsea's hands and moved it along the spot his child had missed.

And with every stroke, she covered ugly spots on his soul with a cheery, bright paint.

His phone beeped with an incoming text message. He fished it out and glanced at the screen. He cringed. His former mother-in-law again.

Doing his best not to let his bitter feelings show on his face, he opened the text, and his insides went cold.

If you want to play the field, give Chelsea to us. We'll raise her as our own daughter.

"I don't wanna beef tacos."

As Chelsea shook her head, Kristina leaned to her and ruffled her blonde hair. Raising two girls had taught her to find compromises. "Okay, what kind of tacos do you want? Because it's gotta be tacos. I set my mind on that." So Chelsea better not suggest muffins or cupcakes for dinner.

The girl stared at her. Kristina stared back. *Gotta be tacos.*

"How about egg tacos? I remember you liked those." Greg stepped to her.

From his proximity, the temperature in her kitchen seemed to increase. And the stove wasn't even on yet.

Chelsea nibbled on her lower lip. "Yeah! I wanna egg tacos."

As he passed Kristina on the way to the stove, he whispered, "Good thing she didn't choose fish tacos, or we'd be in a pickle."

With her heart racing as his breath touched her ear with his whisper, she was in a pickle already. As he snatched her bumblebee-hued apron, her brows shot up. "What do you think you're doing?"

"Why, getting ready to cook." He winked at her.

She eyed him. Hmmm, they went fast from helping to cooking. "Do you know how?"

He chuckled. "Wait till you try them."

Oookay. Warmth rose inside her. The last time a man cooked in her kitchen was… never. Cullen thought cooking was a wife's responsibility and wasn't shy about expressing his opinion. Roman had cooked, yes, but that had been in their parents' kitchen and later in his own house.

Greg fit his palms over her shoulders. "You, Chelsea, and Chip have fun. Rest. You worked hard the entire day. You must be tired."

"Let's go play with Chip, Miss Kristina." The girl tugged at her hand.

Yeah, probably better to stay away from Greg than cook with him. He caused feelings she didn't know what to do about.

Still, she made one more attempt. "Are you going to find everything?"

"I'll do my best." He sent her another of his enigmatic smiles.

She nearly melted like butter on a skillet. Yes, better walk away.

Chelsea and Kristina settled on the soft living room carpet where the girl petted Chip and told him the story about Taco and their new house.

Huh. Cullen had never cared whether she'd worked hard or been tired. He'd always claimed he'd been the one who worked hard, provided for the family, and provided well. On the other hand, she'd done nothing the entire day. Cooking, cleaning, doing laundry, ironing his shirts, gardening, washing his expensive car, helping the twins with homework, and so on didn't really count.

She didn't really count.

How could she be so blind for so long?

She pushed the thought away and smiled as Chelsea chased Chip around the room. Then she moved chairs out of the way so the girl wouldn't bump into them. The child's laughter reminded Kristina of the days her daughters had been little.

Yep, that had been the reason she'd closed her eyes to obvious things. Her daughters.

Kristina found large sheets of paper and drew the contours of a puppy on one of them. Then she put it and coloring pencils on the floor. "Here we go, sweetie. How about you make a beautiful drawing of Chip?"

"Yeah!" Chelsea stopped running and plopped herself on the carpet again. "And Taco?"

"Of course." Kristina smiled as she outlined an elephant. "How can we forget about Taco?"

Mouthwatering scents drifted from the kitchen as she handed the sheet with an elephant to Chelsea, too.

A doorbell made her wince. Roman? Or somebody else?

She leaped to her feet. If it was her brother, she couldn't let Greg see him. Her heart dipped. She'd need to tell Greg about the entire charade eventually, but this would be a bad way for him to find out she'd deceived him.

She took Chelsea's tiny hand. "Let's go see who that is, okay?"

"Okay." The girl ran near her as Kristina hurried to the front door, her little feet tapping against the white-tiled hall.

As Kristina peered into the peephole, she froze. This was much worse.

Cullen.

The bell rang again. Well, she needed to face him, or he'd keep ringing the bell.

She took a deep breath for courage and opened the door.

"Hello, Kristina. Aren't you going to invite me in?" His smile seemed a bit forced. Maybe it was her imagination, but a few more gray hairs sprinkled his black mane, and his eyes, once glittering silvery gray, seemed faded now.

Her voice failing her, she gestured for him to enter, and holding two small blue boxes, he stepped inside.

"Who's this?" He pointed at Chelsea, who hid behind Kristina's back as if feeling the tension.

"This is Chelsea. She is—"

"Doesn't matter. I see you're babysitting. No surprise there. You couldn't find any other job with your lack of qualifications." He handed her the boxes. "From Leanna and Reanna. They asked me to pass along your birthday gifts."

Her heart warmed. She'd rather have her daughters show up themselves, but at least they remembered her birthday was coming up. She took the boxes, then bent to Chelsea. "Sweetie, go see what Chip is doing, so he's not sad alone, okay? And how about you finish coloring Taco?"

"Okay." The girl ran and dropped herself on the living room carpet near the puppy.

Thankful for the open-door plan and keeping the child in her vision, Kristina faced the once-upon-a-time love of her life. And felt nothing toward him. Not even anger.

And maybe that was a good thing. Thanks to God giving her Greg and Chelsea, she was finally making peace with her ended marriage.

He sized her up. "You actually look good. Younger." Disappointment coated his voice.

Huh. Apparently, he was upset she wasn't crying herself to sleep.

She lifted her chin. "Why are you here?"

Cullen spread his hands. "I just told you. To give you gifts. Reanna is busy, and Leanna doesn't want to talk to you."

She winced. Sure enough, he knew to hit where it hurt the most. "Please tell the twins thanks. And thank you for bringing gifts."

Surely, that wasn't the real reason he'd shown up. So, what was?

"I'd do anything for my daughters." He shifted from one foot to the other. "Even consider reconciliation with you."

Her jaw slackened, and she nearly dropped the boxes. "What?"

"I know you don't deserve it." He flicked an invisible speck from his impeccable charcoal-gray suit. "But as a kind man, I can't leave you suffering."

She carefully placed the boxes on the alder side table. It wouldn't be fair to the twins to throw their gifts at her ex. But she was wrong about the lack of anger. So, so very wrong. With lava-hot force, it surged through her veins.

"Get out of here." She kept her voice low so as not to scare Chelsea.

Regret flicked in his eyes so fast she wasn't sure she'd glimpsed it. "I miss you."

Whoa. He'd admitted that?

She tipped her chin. "And I don't miss you. I moved on with my life."

"You did?" His voice rose.

She glanced at the little girl, who stayed on the carpet, but her baby blues widened. "Keep your voice down. You're scaring the child."

He grabbed her arm and squeezed it. Painfully. "You were mine once, and you're going to be again."

CHAPTER ELEVEN

PAIN ERUPTING where Cullen grabbed her, Kristina tried to jerk her hand free.

"Let her go." Greg's calm voice held strength. He reached them in a few quick strides. "I'm not going to repeat myself."

Huh. Even in her apron, he was impressive with his muscular arms and broad chest stretching his black T-shirt and anger flaring his nostrils.

"Miss Kristina!" Chelsea ran to her, and Chip followed with a bark.

Kristina placed a protective arm on the child's shoulder. "It's okay, sweetie. This man is leaving already."

Cullen visibly swallowed as he eyed Greg. "Who are you?"

"I'm Greg Matthews." His jaw twitched. "Kristina's boyfriend."

Whaaaat? Boyfriend? Her knees went weak, and she nearly landed on the floor. But her ex's expression was priceless. As long as she lived, she wouldn't forget it.

Cullen took a few seconds to recover. "That's interesting. Because I'm her husband."

Well, the audacity!

"Former husband." She jerked her chin up. "Who's already leaving."

Barking, Chip jumped up and down.

"If that dog bites me, I'll need a rabies shot." Cullen stepped back.

"It's the poor dog who might get rabies from you," Kristina muttered as she scooped up Chip.

"What?" Cullen narrowed his eyes again.

"I'm saying, farewell." She waved good-bye.

"If you're having difficulty finding an exit, I can help." Greg moved toward him.

"No, I'll let myself out." Cullen's lips thinned. "You'll regret this, Kristina. You all will regret it." As the puppy barked again, Cullen scooted outside.

The roar of his luxury vehicle made her exhale, her shoulders loosening.

"Sorry about this." She sent Greg a guilty glance.

"I'm glad I was here. Um, I overstepped my boundaries by calling you my girlfriend." He drew her into a hug.

She felt wonderfully safe in his arms as she breathed in his enticing cologne, now mixed with the smells of taco shells and fresh vegetables. A pleasant wave spread through her. She wanted to spend forever in his arms, but she had to think about Chelsea and Chip. Reluctantly, she eased out of his embrace.

Yes, he'd lied about being her boyfriend. But she wanted it to be true so badly that it hurt inside.

"That man was mean!" The girl's lower lip trembled.

"Yes, he was, sweetie." Kristina sank to the child and gave her a comforting hug. "But he's gone now."

Greg moved closer to her. "You... don't still have feelings for him, do you?"

"Oh yes, I have strong feelings toward Cullen." She'd laugh if the topic wasn't so sad. "If not for the twins, I'd regret having wasted twenty years of my life on him and be surprised I hadn't figured it out sooner."

He hugged her, sending a wonderful ripple through her, and released her too soon.

Would Cullen stoop so low as to hurt his daughters in revenge? Her insides went cold. He'd always made good on his promises. But she hoped that he did love his children.

She took Chelsea's hand. "Let's go help your daddy finish making tacos."

"Actually, they are done." As Greg wrapped his arm around her shoulder, she forgot everything besides being close to him.

Until a premonition squeezed her heart. No, her ex-husband wouldn't use their daughters.

He'd do something much worse.

Early the next morning, Greg drove to Portland with Kristina in the passenger seat and Chelsea in her booster seat in the back. Kristina was humming some tune on the radio, and so was his daughter.

He joined them, and they sang totally off-key. But he didn't care. Since Kristina had ordered most of the carpet—Chelsea had chosen purple, but Kristina had talked her into a powder blue like Chelsea's eyes—they might as well get some home décor. While he wasn't one for shopping, unless it concerned sports equipment, excitement bubbling inside him suggested he looked forward to the trip.

Her fingers circled the bouquet on her lap, the wonderful aroma of roses spreading in the truck. "You really didn't need to give me flowers. Besides, they'll wither away by the end of the trip."

"I just wanted to see you smile." He'd gladly give her a field of flowers for that.

She turned to him, a smile lighting her brown eyes, and he had his reward. He returned his attention to the road. Then he found her hand and covered her fingers with his.

He'd always thought God meant Sally for him.

After Sally was gone, that should've been it. He'd resolved to raise Chelsea alone.

Could it be God meant Kristina for him, too?

He breathed in the scent of his new car air freshener, mingling with the fragrance of roses and Kristina's subtle perfume. This morning, when they were picking up a few things in the grocery store, Chelsea had chosen this air freshener with some tropical fruit scent, probably mango.

Not buying cherry-scent car air fresheners anymore didn't mean he was going to forget Sally. But trying something different didn't feel like a betrayal to her memory any longer.

He slowed down around a curve.

Not all things were bright and shiny today.

The conversation with his former in-laws and then Kristina's ex-husband rattled him. Obviously, Cullen had wanted her to return. Greg swallowed hard as he passed a car. Could he be sure she didn't have feelings for the guy any longer? After all, Cullen was the father of her children, a man she'd once loved deeply.

Greg squeezed her fingers, and his heart shifted again.

He'd just have to take a leap of faith.

She sent him a guilty glance. "I have to tell you something."

Uh-oh. He tensed. Was she quitting her job already? Or was this about her ex?

"I lied to you." Her voice dipped.

Lied? His jaw tightened as her words jerked his attention her way. Then he turned his focus back to the road.

"I dressed up as my brother so we wouldn't lose you as a client. Roman is on crutches after a motorcycle accident, so he can't do any jobs yet. I know it's no excuse, but I also wanted to help you and Chelsea."

Aha. Air whooshed out of his lungs. "That's all? I figured something was off about Roman. And you slipped up about me and you building the swing."

Their gazes met for a brief moment, and her eyelashes fluttered—was she holding her breath?

"Will you forgive me?"

He sent her an encouraging grin, then returned his attention to the road. "I already have."

Soon, a bit *too* soon, they were in Portland. It was such a beautiful day. A gift from God.

He stilled as he helped Kristina out of the truck. Since when had he considered a day a gift from God?

Since he'd met this woman. He looked into her luminous eyes and knew he was losing his head.

But not so much he'd forget his daughter. He freed Chelsea from the booster seat, and they all walked to the home décor store. There was a skip in his little girl's step as her right hand settled in his palm and her left in Kristina's.

Kristina winked at him. "One, two, three."

They lifted Chelsea, and his daughter squealed. As the soft breeze touched his skin, he felt things kept changing. Was he ready to risk his heart again?

Then he suppressed a frown as he entered the store. Shopping wasn't his forte, but he wanted his girl to have the things she liked once they moved into the house. And for some reason, he wanted Kristina's approval on those things, as well.

Because maybe one day…

No, too early to think of that.

In a few minutes, he forgot why he disliked shopping so much. Chelsea was running around the furniture, hiding behind sofas, and giving herself away by giggles. He'd tried to stop her at first, but soon gave up and just laughed at her antics, as long as she was having fun and didn't run into other customers.

Sure enough, they'd ended up with a maroon couch, a painting with a dog and a kitten, a lamp in the shape of—what else?—an elephant, and other things he probably wouldn't have chosen himself.

Kristina helped Chelsea climb onto the maroon sofa and sat down near her. She hugged a mulberry-hued pillow he suspected was going home, as well. "Well, this was fun."

He dropped onto the cushion on his little girl's other side. "I don't know what I was thinking. It's going to be some strange décor. I should've asked you to make drawings first and then choose pieces accordingly."

"Personally, I like it. It's bright and cheerful. Like you and Chelsea." She grinned at him.

She did have such a wonderful smile….

Snap out of it, man.

He chuckled. "Well, Chelsea, yes. But nobody accused me of being bright and cheerful, not the last two years."

"You're that way to me," Kristina said quietly.

"Maybe because I'm that way *with* you." He stared into her gorgeous brown eyes, forgetting the nearby customers, the salesgirl doing her pitch somewhere.

Kristina's eyes widened, and the air charged with awareness.

"Daddy, look at that chair!" His girl jumped from the sofa and scrambled toward a funky, crimson-red, round-shaped chair.

Kristina rose. "We'd better follow her."

The moment was gone. Stifling his disappointment, he rushed after his daughter and scooped her up before she had a chance to trip over something. "What do you want to eat for lunch, sweetheart?"

"Ice cream! With pistachios!" His child waved.

He glanced back at Kristina helplessly.

She shrugged. "I know it's not a healthy lunch, and I'm not talking like a responsible mother right now. But at least there's no shellfish in ice cream or where it's prepared. And then, once I'm home from celebrating Nai's birthday at The Pancake Shoppe, I can make a healthy meal for you and Chelsea to compensate for it."

"You're awesome, you know that?" He mouthed to her as he placed his kid in the weird chair of her choice.

Kristina looked down. "Well, that's something nobody accused me of before."

"And that's a shame." She'd been deprived of praise and compliments for far too long. Something he fully intended to change.

After an ice-cream parlor visit and a blissful drive home, he unloaded the funky chair, maroon sofa, and boxes in the house. Then he stared at his little family. Well, not family.

Okay, Kristina had become a part of the family, and that filled him with unexpected joy. The moment she left for dinner with her friend, he couldn't wait to see her again. A few hours later, his heart sang as they made tacos with barbacoa together while Chelsea helped them by sitting at the table and playing with Taco.

And as mouthwatering aromas of meat and vegetables spread through the kitchen of her rental, he found his heart aching less and less.

Could he open himself to new love?

Could Kristina?

After working the entire day on Monday laying hardwood flooring in the living room, Kristina and Greg stopped for an early dinner. She spread sheets of paper over a makeshift table—a wooden board topping a large empty paint bucket.

"Apparently, we've gotten different parts of furniture except for the most needed ones." She eyed him.

He nodded. "Did I tell you I missed you on Saturday afternoon and yesterday?"

Kristina laughed softly. She'd only been out with Nai and Reese for two hours before returning home and cooking dinner for Greg and his daughter. "Several times. And again, I'm sorry I couldn't work on Saturday afternoon and Sunday. I do honor Sundays and go to church that day."

"Maybe I could go with you one of these Sundays."

Kristina's mouth tugged with a smile. "I'd like that."

"So, tell me more about this place you went with your friends on Saturday afternoon to celebrate…was it Nai's birthday?"

"Yes, Nai, one of my childhood friends. The Pancake Shoppe on the boardwalk. They have the most amazing pancakes. We need to take Chelsea there some day." Uh-oh. She was getting ahead of herself.

His eyes were hooded as he spread burritos, large flour tortillas filled with refried beans, cheese, lettuce, and pieces of beef fajitas, over the improvised table.

Oh no. She swallowed hard as she lowered herself on the round-shaped armchair. Something was going on with him. "Are burritos okay with you?"

"Totally."

"We have so much great seafood here, but since my daughter can't eat it, I don't go anywhere near seafood, either." His voice tightened as he sat down. "I feel bad not treating you to a lobster or baked salmon or—"

She lifted her hand to stop him. "Burritos are among my favorite foods. It reminds me of the good parts of my childhood. And I admire your dedication to your child."

His gaze softened.

She said grace.

"Amen," he said when she was done.

She took a bite of burrito, but the spicy concoction fell like a stone into her stomach as she looked into his tormented eyes. "What's wrong? You don't like the work we've done? Or is there something wrong with Chelsea?"

A muscle moved in his jaw. "The second. Well, not exactly something wrong with Chelsea. My former in-laws want custody. My mother-in-law told me again this morning when I dropped my daughter off there."

"What?" Her stomach sinking, Kristina lowered her burrito to the table. "Maybe they miss their daughter so much they use Chelsea as a substitute."

His eyes darkened. "Maybe. Sally was their only daughter, a late child when they nearly lost hope to have kids. Chelsea is their only granddaughter. I didn't want to leave Chelsea with them today. But I wouldn't deprive her of seeing them, either. It wouldn't be good for her, and Sally wouldn't want it. And they do have the huge dollhouse she loves so much. Well, it's not about the dollhouse. I could buy her one."

Aching for him, she resisted the urge to reach out to him. "But you can't buy her a new set of grandparents. I see. I'll pray for them, Chelsea, and you. It'll work out."

A muscle in his cheek twitched. Then he finally bit into his burrito. "Do you think so? She nearly died from anaphylaxis under my care."

"And I guess Mrs. Ronfrey doesn't stop reminding you of that." Oops. Her palm nearly flew to her mouth. She should've held her tongue. But his expression indicated she was right. "It's not your fault your daughter is allergic to shellfish, and you've done everything right in that situation."

"Except for bringing her to a restaurant in the first place. I was very confident in my business. But being a single father... I don't know if I'm enough. I don't know whether I'll ever be enough. How will I explain to her how to put on makeup? Or to choose the right outfit? Or..." He visibly swallowed. "Give advice about teenage boys while I want to meet them with a gun when they show up on my porch?"

"God will guide you. Though I can tell you right now, meeting your daughter's future boyfriend with a gun isn't a good idea." She leaned forward. "You're doing a wonderful job. You have a well-adjusted, happy child despite some very tragic circumstances." She paused. Should she say this? "And maybe you won't have to do this all alone. You might meet a woman who'll become a loving wife to you and a wonderful mother to your daughter."

His gaze settled on her eyes, and he put his burrito aside. "What if I already met her?"

She stilled as a warm feeling spread inside her. No, this was dangerous territory. Looking for a distraction, she munched on her burrito again. "Eat. Or your food will get cold."

"Right." He sipped his iced tea.

She managed a few more bites, the tastes of tortilla, meat, cheese, and vegetables mixing on her tongue. "You worry about Chelsea, don't you?"

He nodded as he returned to his meal. "All the time. Don't get me wrong. She's the light of my life. I'm so glad God gave her to me. But I'm so scared she'll get hurt."

"I hate to break it to you, but kids get hurt all the time." Genuine pain in his voice caused her to place her hand on his forearm. "They scrape their knees; they fall. My twins have an allergy to eggs, and, boy, did I find out the hard way how many products contain eggs. And wait till some unrequited love will put tears in their eyes. But they survive. And eventually, they thrive, too."

Her heartbeat increased. As touching him started affecting her too much, she moved her hand.

His eyes warmed. "Thank you. That helps. A lot."

As soon as they put wrappers in the trash, they continued laying the hardwood in the living room. She felt the bond between them strengthen. Not only because they both were parents. She and Cullen were parents of the same children, and she'd never felt so connected to him. Probably because her ex had never worried about Leanna and Reanna even a fraction of how much Greg worried about Chelsea.

And Cullen had never really cared about her dreams. He'd just pretended to, so she'd marry him.

Would Greg care?

She jumped to her feet. "Um, you mentioned how maybe I should've done some drawings of the rooms. Well, I did." Unease tightened her stomach.

What was she thinking? Why would he be interested in that? She had no education, no experience as an interior designer. Just some things she'd studied online when she'd had spare time and twins were at school.

"How awesome!" Interest shone in his eyes. "May I see them?"

She poked her toe at an invisible speck on the floor. "Really?"

"Of course." He rose. "Everything about you interests me. And this is actually the interior of my house we're talking about! And... I want you to like this home."

Her heartbeat stuttered. Did she dare to hope? "Why?"

"Just an idea." A twinkle sparkled in his eye. "I can't wait to see what you came up with."

"You might not like it," she muttered, dashing to her car.

When she returned with the drawings, her stuttering heart now hammered. What if he thought they were horrible? Well, she'd have to endure it and try to do better.

As he studied her ideas, she held her breath.

Then a smile curved his lips. "Wow. You're talented, you know that?"

She released her pent-up breath as she stacked the drawings on the makeshift table, the paper giving a satisfying thwunk when she tapped the edges into order. "You really think so? You don't just say it to be nice?"

"You know, you really need to learn to accept compliments. I love your ideas. All of them." He lifted her up and whirled.

Deliciously dizzy, she closed her eyes.

When he put her down, she could barely find her tongue as she opened her eyes. "I... you... thank you." She needed a distraction fast before she did something crazy. Like kiss him.

Silly to get so attracted to a man just because he'd given her more worth than she'd ever given herself.

But she was hungry for more. Oh yeah, and she needed that distraction. She grabbed the drawings and flipped to the next page.

"Here are some ideas for renovating Ivy's on Spruce, my friend Nai's aunt's bookstore. You're the first to see this."

Bent over the drawings, he rubbed the back of his neck. "I can't speak for your friend, but I think they are awesome."

A warm wave spread inside her. "You're being kind again."

"I'm being honest. You're not just a beautiful and compassionate woman. You're talented, too. It's about time you accept that about yourself." He placed the drawings aside and drew her close.

He brought her hand to his lips and kissed her fingers. Then he turned her hand around and brushed his lips against her palm, then against her wrist.

Her pulse skyrocketed, and her heart fluttered. When his kisses traveled to her forearm, she nearly melted. She should draw back. But she couldn't move or speak or even think straight.

A phone ringing forced itself through her mental fog. Was it his phone? Hers? Her mind cleared a bit. It wasn't her ringtone.

He fished his cell phone from his jeans back pocket.

Then he frowned at the screen. "I'm sorry. This is my former mother-in-law. It might be about Chelsea."

"Of course." She nodded. "You need to talk to her."

He swiped the screen and placed the phone to his ear. "Hello." His eyes widened while he listened. "I'll be right there," he said at last. Then he disconnected.

Cold traveled down her spine. Worry tightening her gut, she tugged at his hand. "What happened?"

A muscle in his jaw twitched. "Chelsea disappeared."

She didn't hesitate. "Let's go find her."

CHAPTER TWELVE

GREG'S FINGERS tightened around the steering wheel as he drove to his former in-laws' place. He'd had a feeling he shouldn't leave his daughter this morning. He had! But she'd been so excited to play with the dollhouse, they'd been so insistent on having her for the day, and he'd been so eager to spend time with Kristina… Why had he let them babysit her?

It was all his fault. Dread pooled in the pit of his stomach.

He prayed like he'd never prayed before.

The moment he pulled up to the curb of Mr. and Mrs. Ronfrey's red brick home, he turned off the engine and rushed inside. Kristina would understand why he didn't open the door for her. Her quick footfalls slapped the cement walk behind him as she kept up. Once again, she was with him in a difficult time, without complaining or asking unnecessary questions.

As he rang the bell, the door flung open. Mrs. Ronfrey's pepper-and-salt bun was skewed to the side and her wrinkled apron—stained in tomato juice—askew. Her pale eyes narrowed.

"You're to blame for this." Her mouth twisted, crinkling the wrinkles around it. "You got her that stupid kitten!"

He drew a shaky breath as anger shot through him, but Kristina's soft touch on his hand soothed his raw nerves somewhat.

"May we come in?" He infused his voice with as much politeness as he possibly could.

He had to find his daughter, and arguing with his former in-laws wouldn't help.

The woman's eyes narrowed to slits, but she stepped aside, letting Greg and Kristina hurry into the house.

Stooping as if under a huge weight, Mr. Ronfrey dragged his feet toward them. He looked like he'd aged a decade today. "Hello, Greg."

Greg gestured toward Kristina. "I'd like to introduce—"

"We know who she is," Mrs. Ronfrey hissed. "I knew you were with her! That's why you let us have Chelsea today!"

"Darling, don't start." His voice tired, Mr. Ronfrey hung his head.

Greg's jaw set in a stubborn line. He could take insults toward himself, but not toward the woman who mattered so much to him. "I'll ask you to treat Ms. Vela with respect." He sent Kristina an apologetic glance. "What's important right now is not our disagreement, but how to find Chelsea."

Mrs. Ronfrey twisted her hands. "Who knows where our poor little girl is?"

Her husband raked his fingers through his hair. Usually combed, it stuck in all directions now. "Her kitten escaped when I was taking out the trash. We offered to get her a new kitten later."

Greg suppressed a groan. "But she wanted Cupcake." Sometimes he couldn't understand how a couple like this could raise such a kind, God-honoring woman as Sally. No wonder she'd never liked talking about her childhood. Well, no time for such thoughts.

Finding Chelsea was a priority.

"When we weren't looking, she probably slid through the front door." The man studied the hardwood floor. "We searched the entire house and the yard thoroughly. She's not here."

Ghastly fingers tightened around Greg's heart and squeezed, but his mind whirled. "I'll call the police. Please print out Missing Person flyers with Chelsea's photo in high resolution. We'll put them up in the neighborhood and start talking to neighbors." The Ronfreys lived in a neighborhood mostly occupied by retirees like themselves, so hopefully, at least some people would be at home even on Monday.

Mrs. Ronfrey blinked. "We don't have a printer."

Kristina stepped forward. "I can ask a friend, Nai, to do that. I'll just need to forward her a photo and description."

He snatched his phone out of his pocket and forwarded her Chelsea's photo. He'd snapped it this morning, in her adorable pink overalls, matching ribbons holding up her pigtails as she hugged Cupcake.

Kristina's phone beeped. She opened the message, nodded, and pushed some buttons. "Done. Mr. and Mrs. Ronfrey, if you don't mind, I'll forward Nai your address, so she can bring the flyers here."

Mrs. Ronfrey didn't say anything, but Greg's father-in-law nodded. "Yes, please. We need to find our granddaughter, and we'll appreciate the help."

Greg spun to the front door. "We can start the search while I call the police."

Near the door, he glanced back. His in-laws stayed in their places.

Kristina, who'd followed him, turned around. "Well, it's probably best you wait right here in case Chelsea returns. I'll post on social media about her disappearance and see if I can get locals to spread the news. If that's okay with you."

Considerate as always, she obviously tried to spare their feelings by giving them an important role in the search when they couldn't move from their places. Yes, this was his Kristina.

What? His Kristina?

No time to think about that.

"Thank you." Mr. Ronfrey nodded.

"Good idea." Greg dialed 911 and darted outside. As he talked to the police officer, he scanned the neighborhood. His gut twisted. Where could his little girl be?

When he disconnected, Kristina gestured to the nearest house. "Let's start here. We can show them the picture on your phone while we're waiting for Nai."

He nodded, and they dashed toward the house.

The conversation with the first neighbor yielded exactly nothing. Worry knifed his heart. He couldn't lose his daughter like he'd lost Sally. He just couldn't.

Kristina's lips were moving, and he realized she was praying.

He sent up a prayer of his own from deep within his soul.

She touched his forearm. "We'll find her. Have faith."

But not despairing was difficult when the second and the third neighbor hadn't seen his child, either. The fourth neighbor didn't answer their knock.

A roar of a motor preceded a car pulling up to Mr. and Mrs. Ronfrey's house. A brunette, wearing glasses and a white sweater that contrasted with her long dark hair and black jeans, climbed out of the driver's seat. Another woman, a tall gorgeous strawberry-blonde, slid from the passenger's seat. He recognized the passenger as Reese, a famous supermodel, who—according to Mrs. Ronfrey—returned to Chapel Cove. But he'd never seen the driver.

He glanced at Kristina. "Nai?"

Her face brightened. "Oh yes. And Reese. Girls!" She took off in that direction.

Thankful for her friends' help, he followed.

After brief introductions, Nai handed them a partial stack of flyers. "I couldn't wait to meet you, but I wish it was under different circumstances. I'll keep the rest of the flyers. Reese and I will start putting these up, with homeowners' permission, of course. Then we'll go to the next street and talk to the people there."

"Thank you." Kristina gave her friends a quick hug. "I already posted about Chelsea's disappearance on social media. Can you give me some support there?"

"Sure thing," Reese and Nai said in unison.

Gratitude expanding his chest, he stepped to them. "Nai and Reese, I appreciate you doing this for me and Kristina."

Nai smiled reassurance. "What are friends for?" Chin tipped, she strode away.

His heart heavy, he headed to the next house, a buttermilk-colored stucco, Kristina by his side. After the ninth house and zero results, he felt as if his insides were ripped out. Sharp pain sliced him inside. But he had to remain strong to continue the search.

The urgency to find his daughter pulsed inside him. Three people they'd talked to volunteered to place flyers in Main Street businesses, and one of the neighbors said he could talk to a local TV station. Chapel Cove seemed to have a caring community, and judging by people's compassionate expressions, they worried about his little girl, too.

As Greg and Kristina walked down the porch of the ninth house, she stilled, one hand grasping the wooden railing. "Hold on. Chelsea was trying to find Cupcake, right? Where would the kitten go?"

Hating to feel helpless, he shrugged. "A tree, a roof? Under a car? There are so many places."

A chill grasped his spine. What if his daughter somehow followed Cupcake up the tree? Or even to a roof if somebody left a ladder nearby? What if she fell from it? She could be badly hurt!

Ice filled his veins.

"Let's not think she fell." Kristina seemed to read his mind again. "How about checking some neighborhood trees?"

Plenty of Douglas firs and maples with an occasional red alder towered over fences. How would they be able to check them all?

"Let's try, okay?" Her gaze softened as she squeezed his arm. "Especially the trees a child could easily climb."

Pulling back his shoulders, he strode forward. "Let's do it."

She called out in a gentle voice as she walked along the first fence, "Chelsea, Cupcake!" Only the murmuring foliage responded.

His heart sank, but Kristina took his hand and twined their fingers as if to show support.

"Chelsea, Cupcake!" he shouted.

While they moved along the third white-picket fence, she lifted her hand. "Hold on. Do you hear it?"

Except for his heart's wild beat, he didn't hear anything. But she didn't move, frozen in one place, so he listened intently.

Finally, he distinguished the low sounds. Meowing and sniffling? Yes! His heart nearly stopped beating, then resumed its wild force.

Could he hope? "Where are they coming from?"

The Oregon white oak in front of a house three blocks from Mr. and Mrs. Ronfrey's place? "That one!"

He dashed to the tree, Kristina behind him, and he made it to the oak fast. He peered intently. First, he couldn't see much beyond the foliage.

Then he spotted pink overalls. His heart nearly leaped out of his chest. "Chelsea!"

"Daddy!" His daughter sniffled. "I'm scaaaared."

Breathing hard, Kristina reached the tree. "Oh, sweetie. Did you follow Cupcake there?"

"Yeah!" His child sniffled again.

"I guess neither one of them can climb down now," Kristina whispered.

He figured as much as he sized up the distance. The branches didn't look too sturdy, but he'd risk it. "Hang on, sweetheart. I'm going to get you in a moment."

"Hold on." Kristina's fingernails cut into his arm. "The branches are small. They're not going to support you. I wish I had Roman's truck and ladders."

His jaw set. He'd done way riskier things in his snowboarding career. And here his child's well-being was on the line. "No matter. I've got to try. Chelsea is frightened. I'm not going to make her wait until the police get here."

Kristina shook her head. "I'm much smaller than you. I might be able to climb high enough to get your daughter."

Yes! Then his stomach tightened. "What if you fall?"

Raising her hand, she touched his face with cool fingertips. "Then you'll catch me. I trust you."

What an amazing woman. Simply amazing. "I wish I trusted myself that much," he muttered. "Do you know how to climb a tree?"

People started gathering, and murmurs rippled through the crowd.

She arched her dainty chin. "There are benefits of growing up with a twin brother. Roman loved climbing trees and fences, and I learned to catch up. Um, I might need a lift."

As he hoisted her up, her body fit perfectly in his arms.

She struggled to get her footing but managed to scale a few branches. "I'll be there soon, sweetie. I'll get you."

"And Cupcake." Chelsea hugged the meowing kitten tighter.

"Of course." Kristina's foot slipped.

He and the people near him gasped.

CHAPTER THIRTEEN

AS KRISTINA caught her balance and pulled herself up to the next branch, admiration rose inside Greg. She didn't have to do this. But she'd gone for it, for his daughter, and maybe a little bit, for him, too.

He was eager to climb after this incredible woman and his daughter, but he forced himself to stay in one place and prayed. After losing Sally, putting his trust in God was difficult, but he needed to make that step.

Nai and Reese ran to him. "What is she doing?"

"Trying to get my daughter and a kitten from the tree." His heart beating fast, he watched her every move.

"Yep. That's our Kristina." Nai linked arms with her friend.

More neighbors gathered.

"Mommy!" His daughter's scream made his breath catch. "Mommy, I'm scared."

Mommy... His throat constricted. Had Chelsea called Kristina "Mommy"?

"I've got you, sweetie. I've got you," was Kristina's soft response.

He didn't remember the last time he'd cried. Even when Sally died, something froze inside him, became icy cold and sharp. But now tears prickled the backs of his eyes. He didn't let him spill. He shouldn't.

He blinked furiously as a new feeling rose inside his chest.

If he could ever see God working in people's lives, this was it.

When Kristina climbed down with his girl in her arms, he sent up a prayer of gratitude.

As applause erupted, he rushed to his precious, precious girls and hugged them. He never wanted to let them go. A meowing kitten protested somewhere close to his chest, so he eased up.

His heart flip-flopped as he held them close. "Sweetheart, you scared me so much."

"Sorry, Daddy." Chelsea's voice was so small, but at least, she was okay.

He let them go and studied their dear, beautiful faces. "You have no idea how much you mean to me. Both of you."

Tears streaming down Kristina's face, she shook visibly.

Everything in him ached to kiss those tears away, but she probably wouldn't want him to with an audience. "Thank you so much for helping my daughter. You did great. It's okay now." Words couldn't express his overwhelming gratitude.

"You see," Nai said quietly. "When Kristina was seven, she fell off a fence and broke her leg. She's been afraid of heights ever since."

Speechless, he stared at Kristina. And she'd climbed the tree for his child.

That was the moment he knew he loved Kristina Vela.

Tuesday afternoon, Greg opened the door of Ivy's on Spruce for Chelsea. *Pink* walls—his daughter was going to love it here—cushioned with books softened the echo of their footfalls, and lazy overhead fans stirred up air sweet with the scent of paper and coffee.

"Scoot inside and choose any children's books you like. I'll read them to you later." His heart still trembled over yesterday's scare.

She scurried inside and then lifted her adorable face. "Do they have books about elephants?"

He adjusted a lavender-hued ribbon on her ponytail. "I sure hope so."

As he followed her to the children's books section, Nai strode to him. Her dark-brown hair, pinned in the back, now shone over an olive-green T-shirt that was combined with black slacks. "Good morning."

"Nai, once again, thank you for your help yesterday. And... do you have any kids' books about elephants? Preferably, of purple color."

Kristina's friend laughed. "I don't know about purple; we'll need to ask Violet's advice on that." She gestured to a purple-clad older woman, pottering around the used book section with a feather duster. "But we do have books about elephants." She led them to one of the bookshelves and pulled out a large book with a blue elephant on the cover and handed it to his daughter.

Something screeched in the distance, and Greg stilled. "What's that?"

"My aunt's parrot."

Oh no.

Chelsea's eyes widened as she clutched the book to her chest. "A pa–arrot? I wanna see it."

Greg cringed. "Sorry."

Nai perched eyeglasses framed in ebony, the color of her hair, on her nose. "How about this? It's a slower time of day, and Violet and Fern can take care of things. I'll show Chelsea the parrot and see if they can have a conversation." She leaned toward him and whispered, "And maybe you and Kristina could have a date."

As much as his heart warmed at the idea, he couldn't let his daughter go. Not after yesterday. He shook his head. "Thank you, but that's okay."

"Daddy, I'm not gonna go anywhere. I promise." Arms crossed primly over the book in front of her, Chelsea tipped her head up at him. Her eyes now serious, she could have been a miniature librarian about to lecture him.

"I'm not going to let her out of my sight. Honest." Nai laid a hand on the girl's shoulder.

Trust me.

The words appeared in his mind.

"Pretty-pretty please?" A familiar stuck-out lip made him smile.

Lord, I trust in You. Please keep my daughter safe in Your care.

"You're a great friend." He handed Nai the payment as she rang up the book.

"I know." She grinned and leaned forward. "Is it okay to treat your daughter to a glass of apple juice and a brioche filled with chocolate? Kristina's favorite, by the way."

He nodded with enthusiasm. Something told him Chelsea would be bringing him back to this place in the future. "Kristina has friends as amazing as she is."

Nai laughed. "Go, or I might change my mind."

He explained about Chelsea's shellfish allergy and how serious that was. Then he handed Nai EpiPens and clarified how to use them.

She nodded. "I'll make sure she won't come anywhere close to shellfish."

Then he gave his little girl a tight hug. "I'll be back soon, okay?"

After leaving the store, he called Kristina. "If you'd like to take a break from work, how about we check out that amusement park Roman—I mean, *you*—told me about?"

Kristina's heart hammered as Greg drove her to the amusement park. Let's face it, she went dizzy around him without wobbling in a bucket in the air. But when she'd been thirteen, she'd wanted to do something crazy. While this probably didn't qualify, it was a start.

"Reese and Nai went to the amusement park a lot when we were kids. But I didn't join them, though I hated to miss out on all the fun. After I fell off the fence, even thinking of heights gave me a sick feeling." Her stomach clenched.

As much as she loved being with Greg, maybe she'd be better off celebrating Reese's birthday with her and Nai. But Reese had canceled earlier that morning, preferring to have dinner with Heath instead. Not that Kristina could blame her. Both Heath and Reese used to have strong feelings for each other before Reese had chosen her career over love and left Chapel Cove. Now it seemed those feelings returned full force.

And so did Kristina's "love" for heights.

"You remembered the pain of falling." Greg sent her a concerned glance as he passed a black SUV. "I should've thought of it. My bad. Maybe this wasn't such a great idea. Let's do something else."

Though her hands trembled slightly, she threw her shoulders back. "No, I want to do it. I wanted to for some time. I just needed a push in the back, I guess."

And the support of a strong, understanding man. She twisted in her seat to stare at his handsome profile.

The drive to the shore didn't take long.

Her insides shook as she walked to the Ferris wheel, but Greg's fingers tightened around hers made it easier to breathe. Her heart hammering, she settled into a bucket that was as wobbly as her stomach. When the attendant locked her and Greg into a seat, her gut twisted, and bile rose inside her.

Oh no. The last thing she needed was to lose her stomach's contents in the air. Greg was right. It wasn't a great idea.

Lord, please help me.

Greg found her hand again. "It's going to be fine. God's got you."

His touch, his glance, but mainly his words soothed her raw nerves. She managed a shaky nod.

She gasped as the bucket lifted in the air with the soft whoosh. Eyes wide, she breathed fast as if she'd run a marathon. The attendant moved to the next couple, and the rocking of the bucket made her squeeze Greg's fingers.

His eyes were warm, understanding, though by now she was probably squeezing his fingers nearly enough to break them.

"You're going to love this. The rush being in the air gives you is incredible."

"I'll take your word for it," she squeaked as the wind threw her hair around her face.

Then they moved higher and higher still, and her eyes went huge. Her nausea dissipated, and air filled her lungs. She was as high as she'd ever been in her life.

And... Amazingly, she felt safe—absolutely safe. Adrenaline surged in her veins.

Spilling before her, the serenity of the ocean, the beauty of God's creation amazed her more than ever.

Greg eased closer to her. "Do you like it?"

Her chest expanding, she nodded. She'd cherish this moment forever. "I love it."

Maybe God had sent her Greg to show her a path to the woman she could become, no matter what age, to make her see she could strive for her old dreams instead of keeping them buried.

And submerged in his aquamarine eyes, she saw a totally new dream for herself, too.

A very simple dream, really, but an amazing one. *To love and be loved.*

As exhilarating as the ride was, even more, she wanted to be in his arms. Yes, she was a goner.

When buckets made their descent and theirs finally touched the ground, a slight sting of disappointment surprised her. Who'd think?

Later, they strolled along the shore, hand in hand, and the breeze played with her hair. Despite the cool air, warmth spread through her body at his touch.

"Kristina..." He stopped and turned to her. Then his gaze slid to her lips.

Her heart jumped.

Was he...

Was he going to kiss her?

He wrapped his hands around her waist and brought her close. She forgot how to breathe.

"I wanted to tell you for some time..." His breath caressed her skin.

Somehow, she had the presence of mind to lift her hand. "No. You shouldn't say anything." She tried to remember all the reasons she couldn't fall for this man, but when he looked at her like that, they escaped her mind.

"You're right. I should stop talking." He stroked her face with his fingertips, and emotion glowed in his eyes. "Because I want to kiss you so badly I can't stop myself any longer."

Awareness shot through Kristina. She should move back. She *really* should move back.

Instead, she rose on her tiptoes as high as she could and slipped her arms around his neck. Sometimes being so petite had disadvantages. Thankfully, it didn't seem to bother Greg. He dipped his head and claimed her lips with his.

As he deepened the kiss, she left the world of self-doubt and suffering and entered a new, incredible world where she was cherished just the way she was. Wonderful sensations spread through her as she drank in his kiss, so thirsty for his love. She felt she'd stop breathing if he let her go even for a moment.

And with every second, it was getting better and better as butterflies fluttered tender wings in her stomach. She was falling in love with this man, probably was more than halfway through, and she didn't care. She just needed him to kiss her like that, to hold her like that.

And she desperately, desperately needed him to love her.

Yes, he was attracted to her. This much was clear. But she couldn't settle for a mutual attraction. She wanted more, much more.

He liked her all right. But with his past heartache would he ever love her? Or would he break her heart like Cullen had?

In the evening, Kristina danced around the kitchen as she checked on chicken fajitas with pepper and onions on the stove. She lifted the cover from the pan with Mexican rice and smiled at the bright orange color and delicious scent of rice, onions, and tomatoes.

Then she scooped out mint-green avocadoes, added mayo and tomatoes chopped in tiny pieces, and mixed it all up. Okay, now a little bit of spices and salt. Guacamole was ready.

Her heart humming a cheerful song, she couldn't wait for Greg and Chelsea to show up. She wanted the evening to be peaceful and pleasant. And let's face it, she was eager to see Greg.

Very much so.

Oh, she could still feel the gentleness of his embrace as he held her, those butterflies fluttering in her stomach when he'd kissed her, and she was so eager for him to kiss her again....

Uh-oh.

She'd better pay attention to those fajitas instead of daydreaming before she burned them. She lowered the heat under the skillet but couldn't stop her heart from beating fast.

Should she tell him that her birthday was tomorrow? No, then he'd feel obligated to buy her a present, come up with the way to celebrate it, and she didn't want him to feel that obligation. Besides, she'd already promised Nai and Reese to meet up for coffee and cake at Ivy's on Spruce café. It had been kind of Nai to invite her in the first place.

Kristina's phone rang. She fished it out of her jeans back pocket and smiled at Greg's number on the screen. "Hello, Greg."

"Hello, dar—Kristina. We're on our way. Can't wait to see you." There was a pause. "And I'm not saying it just because you're cooking dinner. I told you I'd be happy to cook it."

She smiled. "How about you show your chef's skills tomorrow while I play with Chelsea?"

"I'll be happy to."

"Can't wait to see you, too." As she disconnected, she nearly slapped herself on her forehead. She couldn't meet him in a stained apron over old jeans and a faded T-shirt, could she?

She turned off the heat under her fajitas and dashed into the bedroom, then to her closet. What to wear?

She zoomed in on the ivory knee-length dress Reanna had given her for her thirty-ninth birthday.

Thank You, Lord.

She slid into the dress and zipped it up. Elegant velvet hugged her better than her baggy things. Cullen always said she was frumpy.

She lifted her chin. Cullen didn't rule her life or her mind anymore.

A totally different woman looked at her from the mirror than the one who'd moved to Chapel Cove. A woman whose gaze had regained its confidence and whose lips could smile easily.

She touched those lips with a wine-hued lipstick, brushed her hair, and sprinkled on a few drops of perfume. The doorbell rang. Well, that would have to do.

She rushed to the door and froze at the huge bouquet of red roses in Greg's hands, as well as a large box with *the* chocolate cake. Chelsea was holding a much smaller box of cupcakes.

Recovering, Kristina waved them in.

"That's very sweet, but what's the occasion?" She gestured to the roses as she led them to the dining room. Did he find out somehow that tomorrow was her birthday?

"Um, the opportunity to see you?" He placed the cake on the thankfully big dining table. "You look amazing." He leaned to her. "Smell amazing, too."

She rescued the cupcakes from Chelsea's hands and put the box on the table, as well. Then she fetched a vase with water and arranged the roses in the middle of the living room coffee table. Their wonderful aroma spread through the room. "Do you mean my perfume or fajitas?"

"I mean you." Admiration shone in his eyes.

Warmth spread inside her. Did she forget to turn off the stove? She winced but couldn't move.

Chip's bark threw her out of her daze as the puppy ran to greet his guests. "Oh, no, no, no. You're not going anywhere near the food."

"I brought him a toy." Chelsea reached inside her miniature pink purse with authority.

"Good idea. Play with the puppy while we lay the table, sweetheart." Greg rearranged his daughter's cute pigtails. "Then you'll wash your hands, and we'll eat."

"Okay, Daddy." Happy to oblige, the girl chased after the puppy.

"Sorry I didn't have a chance to set the table," Kristina whispered.

"Are you kidding? You made all that food, and you're apologizing? Give yourself some credit. Thank you for all you've done." He placed his hands on her shoulders.

In such close proximity to him, she nearly forgot to breathe. "It's just...Cullen would get upset if the plates weren't on the table by the time he was home."

His eyes darkened. From anger? Compassion? "I'm not Cullen."

"I'm grateful for that." His face heated it up as his gaze roamed it. When he reached up and brushed a strand of hair behind her ear, she struggled for rational thought. "You must be hungry. Let's get that table ready."

Still, disappointment squeezed her rib cage when he let her go.

Working in tandem, they brought plates, glasses, utensils, and napkins to the table. And every time their hands touched, she felt something akin to an electric jolt, but a pleasant one.

Soon she loaded their plates with food.

"Chelsea!" He strode to the living room and scooped up his daughter. "Let's go wash your hands."

When they all—minus Chip—sat at the table, Kristina took Greg's and Chelsea's hands and bowed her head.

"I'll say grace." Greg's voice was quiet. "Dear Heavenly Father, thank You for this food we're about to eat and please bless it. Please bless the hands that prepared it. Please keep Kristina and Chelsea safe in Your care. And thank You so much for sending Kristina into our lives. Amen."

She was touched, very touched by his words. Gratitude swelled her heart. She was forever grateful to God for sending her Greg and Chelsea, as well.

Greg filled everybody's glasses with iced tea from the pitcher, then cut Chelsea's fajitas and peppers into tiny pieces. Fingers wrapped around the smooth, cold surface of her glass, she watched them take a few bites of fajitas and a couple of forkfuls of rice. Her stomach was a little tense. Cullen had criticized her cooking way too often.

"Yummy!" the girl said around a mouthful of chicken and vegetables.

"I agree." Greg carefully wiped a spot on his daughter's cheek. "Absolutely delicious. Plus, add to all your other great qualities, you're a fantastic cook."

Yay! Relaxing a bit, Kristina gave her food its due.

Her phone rang somewhere in her bedroom. She grimaced and ignored it. It went silent and then rang again.

"Someone's calling you." Chelsea tilted her face expectantly.

Sighing, Kristina rose to her feet. "I'll have to take that. Might be one of my daughters." What if Leanna finally decided to talk to her and wish her happy birthday? Hope fluttered inside her.

"Of course." Greg nodded.

"I'll be quick."

In her bedroom as she picked up her phone, her heart dropped at the name on the screen. Cullen. She should just ignore his call. Then she ground her teeth. He wouldn't stop calling, and if she didn't answer, he'd show up.

Might as well get this over with. Besides, what if it was about their daughters?

"Hello, Cullen." Huh. Her voice was confident, if somewhat cold. "If this isn't about Leanna or Reanna, I don't want to hear it."

"Whoa, dear wife." How arrogant he sounded! "Well, this is about Chelsea."

"Chelsea?" Her fingers loosened on the phone, and her heart sank further as she fumbled not to drop the slim plastic.

"I'll get straight to the point. I'm the Ronfreys' new lawyer. They want full custody of Chelsea. I'll do everything to get it for them."

No, no, no. She wrapped her fingers tight around the cell phone, the edges pinching into her skin. "Impossible. They'd have to prove Greg is an unfit father, and he's a great father."

Cullen tsked. "Oh, marriage with me taught you nothing. Truth can be twisted. I'll dig up any little speck of dirt on your beloved

Greg, anything I can find in his life, and I'll make it look much worse. I'll put his name through the mud publicly. For example, do you know he used to date a lot before he married? A player with no regard for women's feelings. Or that he was a snowboarder who traveled high slopes? A risk-taker who could lose his life easily. I'm sure I'll find much more than that, and I'll drag the custody case out for a long, long time. And meanwhile, he and his daughter will suffer. So sad."

"You wouldn't do this." She straightened her spine.

"You know me better than that. How often have I lost a case?" If possible, his voice became even more conceited.

Her knees wobbling, she sank onto the bed. Yes, she knew him better. He was one of Portland's most successful divorce lawyers. "What do you want?"

"You. It might come as a surprise to you. It is to me. But the house doesn't feel the same without you. It's just... empty. Everything is... empty."

"We're done." She swallowed hard. She finally learned to stand tall, and her ex-husband still tried to jerk the carpet from under her. To lose Greg and Chelsea... Now *her heart* felt empty. And she realized something. Something so simple and so profound that her life would never be the same. Something that left her with no doubts. "I love him."

After a sharp whistle, a long pause stretched like her ready-to-snap nerves.

Then Cullen came back on the line, his tone brisk. "Hmmm. I didn't anticipate that. How soon you forgot about me, about your vows to me."

"Cullen!" She exploded. "*You* broke those vows."

"And *I'm* trying to mend it all now. *I* am, not you, apparently. I'll make sure our daughters know about your unforgivable behavior."

She rubbed her forehead. "Our daughters are grown-up enough to think for themselves. Good-bye."

"Hold on. If you love him, are you ready to see him suffer? From what I heard, he adores his daughter. Think about it. Think well."

The line went dead.

She placed the cell phone on the nightstand and, for a few long moments, stared at its blurring form. Then she hid her face in her hands. What could she do now? Cullen might not succeed in getting the Ronfreys full custody of Chelsea, but he'd fulfill his promise to make Greg suffer. No doubt about it.

Something soft touched her hands, and she moved them away from her face.

Chelsea stood in front of her, her baby blues big. "Mommy, are you okay?"

A huge lump formed in Kristina's throat. She'd been so deliriously happy to hear that *mommy* word yesterday. She'd come to love this child as if she were her own. She hugged the little girl. "Yes, sweetie."

Then Kristina lifted her face.

Concern narrowing his eyes, Greg stood nearby, arms folded across his chest, back braced against the doorjamb. "Sorry to interrupt you. Chelsea—*we*—worried about you."

Her limbs heavy, she forced herself to get up from the bed. She looked at him, committing his image to memory. Soon, she'd have to make a decision. If she knew her ex, and she knew him well, he wouldn't give her much time.

She stretched her lips into a smile. She shouldn't ruin their dinner. "Let's go eat before the food gets cold."

They walked back to the dining room.

Her appetite was gone, but she managed to swallow a few bites and flush them down with iced tea, barely sensing any taste.

After placing Chelsea on the couch to watch cartoons, Greg helped her clean the table.

"What's wrong?"

"Nothing." A lump grew bigger in her throat as she placed the last dish in the dishwasher. "Let's go check on Chelsea."

"Nothing?" He took her hand in his. "Are you sure? You looked different after that phone conversation. Anything I can help you with?"

Well, she'd never make it as an actress. Amazing she'd briefly managed to pass herself for Roman. "I'm sure. Just tired."

He winced. "You've been working hard on my house today. I should've been the one to cook."

Was he for real? They needed to start fighting about something, anything. That would make her decision easier. Because now, all she could think about was how much she wanted to be with him.

"I was glad to cook it. I was happy to share it with you and your daughter." She freed her hand from his.

His lips pressed tight. Then they went to the living room.

A dandelion-colored blanket wrapped around her, Chelsea was sleeping on the couch, Chip in the land of dreams right beside her. So much love filled Greg's expression as he tucked the blanket around her.

And that gesture made Kristina's decision not difficult at all.

Her throat constricted. Greg belonged with his daughter. She wanted so badly to become part of this little family, but that might never happen. And in the interim, she couldn't make these two wonderful people experience pain.

She gripped his hand and led him back to the dining room where they could talk in hushed voices but still see Chelsea. "I need to tell you something."

"I need to tell you something, too." He stopped in the dining room. "But I'd like to do this first. I've been thinking about it the entire evening."

Before she had a chance to say anything, he drew her close and claimed her lips, turning her as light as a feather. An incredible wave swept her up, a whirlwind of sensations, and banished all rational thought. Every cell in her body sang with delight, and her pulse skyrocketed. This kiss was even better than the first one, and she didn't think it could get any better.

When she finally came up for air, she couldn't move for a few seconds, still lost in that amazing world of being close to him. But as things came back into focus, so did her conversation with Cullen.

Her gut twisted.

How could she walk away from Greg? Even all her willpower might not be enough.

He stroked her face with his fingertips. "Kristina, what I wanted to tell you is… I've never thought I'll feel this way again. You brought so much joy into Chelsea's and my life. Your kindness… Your readiness to help… Even your shyness are so endearing. You came into our lives when my outlook on the future was gloomy. And now… I don't know how to say it. You just make my heart beat faster, and I'm happy when I'm around you."

Oh, how she longed to hear these words! Every word caressed her soul and struck it at the same time. She lifted her hand. "Greg, I've got to tell you—"

"I love you, Kristina." Emotion gleamed in his eyes.

And he just made her decision so much more difficult again. Her breath caught in her throat.

If not for Cullen's demand, everything in her would be overflowing with happiness. She really needed to gather that willpower again, every ounce of it.

She stepped back and hugged her middle. "No, no, no." She couldn't breathe.

His body jerked, and he raked a hand through his hair. "Okay, not the reaction I expected. You might not feel the same for me, but I'm willing to wait. You're worth it."

Finally, she managed to get some air in her lungs. "I can't be with you. I might even leave for Portland soon."

CHAPTER FOURTEEN

PAIN SLICED Kristina.

"Why?" Greg's face contorted. Then it grew incredulous. "Chelsea? You know I come as a package deal, but... You don't want to raise somebody else's child?"

Yes, Chelsea was the reason, but not in the way he thought. "I adore her. I really do. But Cullen..." No, she couldn't tell Greg, or Greg would try to talk her out of what she was about to do.

"Wow." His jaw slackened. "You're going back with your ex. So you still have feelings for him. Besides the regret you mentioned."

She rubbed her temples. "It's not that."

"Can I do anything to change your mind?" The misery in Greg's eyes tore at her.

Emotion closed her throat. So she simply shook her head.

"I love you. I love you very much. And I thought…" He took her trembling hands. "I thought you had strong feelings for me, too. You said—"

"I know!" She needed to stop this, or she wouldn't be able to walk away. "Some things are more important than our own happiness. See, when you're a parent, you put the well-being of the child higher than your own. I have to do this."

And she got attached to his sweet kid so much she'd give up her happiness for Chelsea's and Greg's.

His fingers encircled her hands, their warmth reaching deep inside her. "But your daughters are grown-up. Why do you have to go back with Cullen for their sake? Because he's turning them against you? Maybe I can talk to them, make them see the truth."

"It's more than that. And more complicated." She drew a deep breath for courage, and the familiar scent of his woodsy cologne assaulted her nostrils.

She couldn't tell him, couldn't make him choose between her and his daughter. She wouldn't let him go through this. She loved him too much.

He drew her close. "Just know that, whenever you change your mind—and I hope with all my heart you will—Chelsea and I will be here. Waiting for you. Loving you. Always."

"Daddy, Mommy!" Rubbing her eyes, Chelsea ran to them.

"Miss Kristina has to leave us soon. But maybe she'll come back. We'll be waiting for her in Chapel Cove. Right, Chelsea?"

The girl nodded. "You don't want to be my mommy anymore?" A tear sliding down the child's cheek scraped Kristina raw.

She eased her hands out of Greg's and squatted in front of the girl. "I'm sorry, sweetie. I'm so sorry." Tears burned the backs of her eyes, but she held them back. She had to be strong for the girl's sake.

"This is for you." Chelsea ran for her little pink purse, then opened it and took out a folded piece of paper. She handed her a drawing.

It had a tall man, a woman with dark shoulder-length hair in a yellow dress, and a blonde girl with pigtails and a pink sweater aside a dog, a kitten, and an elephant. The animals were nearly the size of humans, but Kristina didn't mind.

The girl pointed to the drawing. "It's you, me, Daddy, Chip, Cupcake, and Taco. A family." Then she handed her the toy elephant. "Taco wants to stay with you. We love you, Miss Kristina."

A lump grew to a gigantic size in her throat. How could she walk away? But she had to for this innocent girl and her father.

Kristina hugged Chelsea and breathed in her sweet mango scent. "I love you, too, sweetie. Very much."

When she straightened out, Greg hugged her gently. She savored those moments to go over later when she'd be nursing her broken heart.

"Remember what I said," he whispered in her ear. "Tomorrow, a year, five years from now, we'll be waiting for you. Come back to us. Do you hear me?"

His breath caressed her ear while his words touched her soul. A few more such minutes, and she wouldn't be able to leave them. She already felt as if parts of her were ripped out.

She eased back. A handsome, caring, young guy like that... It would be easy for him to meet somebody younger and prettier than Kristina and without a vengeful ex-husband. "Move on with your life, Greg. You'll find somebody better soon enough."

"You don't get it, do you? There's no one better than you for me. You're it. Now and forever."

She couldn't hold back her tears any longer, but she couldn't let them see her cry, either. Chip ran to her, and she scooped him. He licked her face, and she closed her eyes. When she opened them, she had to blink furiously. "Chip, you'll be going with this family now. Behave and do your best not to chew too much of their furniture."

Chip whined as if she were betraying him as she leaned and handed him to Chelsea. "Take good care of him, sweetie."

"Yes, Mom—Miss Kristina."

Miss Kristina again... She straightened out and looked somewhere past Greg. Looking in his eyes was too painful. "I'll get his things in a few moments."

Too many good-byes in one evening. And each one was shattering her heart. "Farewell, Greg. Good-bye, sweetie."

When Greg, Chelsea, and Chip quietly left her house, they took her heart with them, aching and bleeding.

The next day, Greg took his daughter to the playground, then to the ice-cream parlor, and even suggested getting a pet squirrel, though he didn't know where he'd get the squirrel. But Chelsea only shook her head, her pigtails jumping. Then she kept pouting, her baby blues sad.

A vise squeezed his heart. As heartbroken as he was over Kristina's leaving, seeing his little girl like this simply tore him apart. At this point, probably even if he suggested getting a live elephant, she wouldn't cheer up.

To top it off, he was up for a custody battle. He cringed. He needed to meet with his lawyer in Portland tomorrow. He'd postponed it long enough already, though he usually wasn't one to procrastinate.

Later in the day, as he helped her settle on a swing in his backyard, memories flooded his mind. How he and Kristina had looked at each other while pushing his daughter on the swing. How he'd held Kristina when she'd painted the top spot on that patio door. How he'd kissed her.

"Daddy, I miss Mommy. Chip is missing her, too," Chelsea's voice was unusually quiet.

"I miss her, as well. With all my heart." He looked into his daughter's huge baby blues.

Had he made a terrible mistake falling in love with Kristina, letting his child get attached to her? He brushed aside a strand of soft hair from her forehead, wishing he could spare her the pain much more than he'd wish to spare himself.

Her face brightened. "Then let's go get her, Daddy."

"It's not so simple, sweetheart." His heart ached. "She has two daughters whom she loves. She wants to be with them."

And with the man who'd mistreated her for over two decades. But Greg didn't add that, of course. He could get why Cullen would want his ex-wife back. Kristina was incredible. But why would *she* want to go back? Maybe she'd never stopped loving him.

Greg stifled a flare of jealousy.

Chelsea's eyes widened. "But, Daddy, Miss Kristina said God gives us big hearts. Her heart is big enough to love us, too."

"Oh, sweetheart." How could he explain that Kristina had chosen her other family over them? It was her right, but letting her go wasn't easy.

In fact, it was killing him.

The next day, the doorbell made Kristina lift her heavy head from the pillow. All that crying left her head and everything else in her body feeling as if someone filled it with lead.

She'd canceled her birthday celebration with Nai, Reese, and Roman. And Reanna had called her in the morning to wish her happy birthday and say she regretted she couldn't come from Portland. Leanna hadn't returned her calls, but Kristina was too spent to be upset about it like she normally would be.

If that was Greg, she wasn't going to open up.

Nooooo.

Or maybe?

The doorbell rang again. "Hermanita, this is your darling brother, and he's not going away. Open up, please." Roman's shout affected her eardrums.

She groaned. Sometimes that brotherly love could be too much. But she knew her twin. He'd camp out on her porch if needed. And frankly, today was his birthday, too. No matter how miserable she was, the least she could do was to wish him happy birthday. She sat up straight and slipped her feet into the place where her slippers were supposed to be, missed them, cringed, then found them.

Grimacing, she dragged herself to the front door and opened it.

Roman's jaw slackened as he stepped inside. "Whoa. This is worse than I thought. You look horrible."

She should've let him camp out on her porch. "You really know how to cheer a woman up."

"Okay. Oops." He handed her a box of chocolate. "Happy Birthday! I have another present for you, but I couldn't bring it." He gestured at his crutches with a frown. "An assortment of paintbrushes, a saw, and a shiny box with screwdrivers wait for you at my house. I hoped you'd like this more than a pretty dress or diamond earrings."

"You know me well. And thank you." She accepted the chocolates and placed them on the coffee table. She forced a smile. Yeah, this was a very *happy* birthday. Not! "I also have a large collection of tools for you as a present. I'll drop them off at your house later. I wouldn't want you to drag it on your crutches."

"You're the best, hermanita." Roman gave her a brotherly hug, then stiffened, drawing back.

Crutches thumped against tile as he walked into the dining room and dropped on the chair he'd made. "I nearly fell when you texted me yesterday that you broke up with Greg and went back to Cullen. Did you get hit by a brick?"

Huh. She folded her arms on her chest as she sank onto the nearest chair. "No, but if you continue like this, you're going to get hit by a skillet."

"Well, if no brick's involved and Cullen simply brainwashed you, my job is to brainwash you right back." He leaned forward, elbows braced on his knees, hands clasped before his chin. "I've never seen you as radiant as after you met Greg. You're in love with him. Yes, you adore Leanna and Reanna, but it's time for you to think about your own happiness. They'll understand."

"It's not about that. Though it's part of my decision." She covered her face with her hands. Then she removed them and straightened up. She'd never kept secrets from her twin, and she wasn't about to start. "Here's what happened. But would you like me to make you some coffee first?"

"I want to know what's happening in your life to make you this miserable much more than I want coffee." Roman's brows drew together.

She hugged her middle. "It hurts so much. Probably as much as when you lost Aileen."

She could never understand how Aileen, who'd left Chapel Cove for Portland to become a pastry chef, could forget her brother and marry someone else. When Roman and Aileen dated, they'd seemed so much in love. When their family received the invitation to Aileen's wedding years later, Roman had taken his motorcycle and driven somewhere all night. Kristina and her mother had been terrified and hadn't slept until he'd returned. After a few years, Roman started dating a lot but never settled down. Then Aileen had shown back up in Chapel Cove to take over her cousin's failing pastry shop, with a son and a few pets in tow.

Roman's face darkened. "It's in the past. I survived."

Something in his eyes told Kristina not everything was in the past. But the morning he'd shown up after that crazy motorcycle ride, he'd asked her not to talk about Aileen, and Kristina hadn't. Until now.

A doorbell made her wince. "It'd better not be Greg."

Her brother shrugged. "Sorry to disappoint you, but it's probably Nai and Reese. I called them. I figured I might need reinforcements."

She glared at him as she forced herself to get up. "I just might go get that skillet. I wanted to be alone!"

"No, you didn't." He gave her an innocent look.

She snorted and went to open the door. Nai and Reese walked inside, Reese holding a box with a chocolate cake—or rather *the* chocolate cake that started all her troubles rather than soothed them as she'd hoped. Nai hugged a box from which the delicious scent of brioches teased Kristina's nostrils.

Nai stared at her. "Whoa."

Kristina's lips pursed. "Don't tell me I look horrible, or you'll be leaving."

Her friend nibbled on her lower lip. "Okay. I see. Well, you look great." She didn't sound very persuasive. "Happy Birthday. Roman! Happy Birthday, Kristina!"

Roman tipped the brim of an imaginary hat. "Thank you, ladies."

Kristina's eyes misted. "Does it look like a *Happy* Birthday? I just broke up with the person I'm crazy about."

"Um, I'll go make coffee." Reese scooted in the kitchen's direction.

"I'll cut the cake." The thumping of crutches followed her.

"And I…" Nai dropped into a chair. "I'll just be here for moral support. What?" She blinked innocent owlish eyes behind her darling glasses. "That's the most important part."

Soon, everybody was sitting at the table, enticing aroma rising from the coffee cups, a slice of rich chocolate cake on each saucer side by side with a brioche, the one with chocolate filling on Kristina's plate, of course. Kristina didn't have much of an appetite even for her favorite dessert, but she couldn't send her friends away. She breathed in the delicious scents. Well, maybe a tiny piece.

Roman said grace.

As the utensils clicked against porcelain, Kristina told them about her conversation with Cullen.

"That's a relief." Roman swirled his coffee. "For a moment there, I thought you lost your mind."

"Really?" Kristina thumped her cup on the table. "I'm suffering here. Another joke like that, and you won't be just eating the cake. You'll be wearing it, too."

"You, guys, are adorable." Nai licked frosting from her spoon. "But we need to see how we can remedy the situation. My boss has some connections in Portland. We'll find a great lawyer to match your Cullen."

Roman rubbed his forehead. "Greg's former in-laws go to our church. I've been attending the entire time you were away, so I know Pastor Don well. I'll have a conversation with him. Maybe he can talk some sense into them."

Kristina straightened in her chair, sloshing the cup in front of her as fragile hope stirred inside her. "Do you think it's possible?"

He nodded. "Well, let's pray about it. We'll go from there."

"I knew there was a reason I love you." After shoving back her chair, the legs scraping against the tile, Kristina ran around the table and hugged him.

"Coming from someone who wanted to hit me with a skillet minutes ago." He polished off the rest of his cake.

"Kristina, maybe you should talk to the Ronfreys, too." Reese was putting a dent in her slice of cake fast. But then, she didn't have to diet any longer.

It dawned on Kristina. "That's right. What if they're just afraid I'd stop them from seeing Chelsea if Greg marries me? Not that he actually proposed or anything." Warmth tingled her cheeks.

"Yeah, kinda hard to do it when you were kicking him out of your life." Nai poked the tines of her fork at her slice, coming away with barely a crumb.

"I had a good reason for it." Kristina looked around the table at the people she loved so much. "I feel better. Thank you so much, you all. Okay, you can wish me Happy Fortieth Birthday now."

"Fortieth?" Roman gave her another innocent look. "If we weren't twins and obviously I can't forget my own age, I'd never give you a day over…" He paused.

"Careful, hermano. Careful." Kristina narrowed her eyes.

"Over twenty-five. And I know a certain young man who probably wouldn't give you a day over twenty."

Kristina shook her head. She could understand why he was so popular with women, though she wished Aileen hadn't crushed his heart badly enough to make it close to new love. "You don't change."

"You wouldn't want me to."

She thought about Roman's birthday gift and slapped herself on the forehead. The paintbrush! "Girls, remember, today is the day we were going to dig out the treasures we hid at thirteen after we made our list of things to do before forty." She turned to Roman. "Sorry, us girls only."

"Totally fine with me." He lifted his hands in a mocking surrender.

Something tender uncurled inside Kristina as she thought about the item she'd put in a tin box as part of her dream. A paintbrush wrapped in a picture of a beautiful home, signifying the job she wanted and the place for a family.

She scooped a bite of the delicious dessert. Was there really a chance for her, Greg, Chelsea, and their pets to be a family? Or was she just kidding herself?

A day later…

"Are we going to go get my new mommy?" Chelsea asked from the backseat.

Pain knifed Greg's heart as he threw a glance at his child. He returned his attention to the road. "No, sweetheart."

They were driving to Portland to discuss the upcoming custody hearing with his lawyer, but he still didn't know how to explain to Chelsea that her grandparents were trying to take her away from him.

"Why?" Whiny notes grated his already frayed nerves.

He changed lanes to pass a red SUV. Maybe his daughter was onto something. And if he'd been the type to give up easily, Chelsea wouldn't have existed. Given his prior reputation as a player, he'd spent months before Sally gave him a chance.

He called Kristina on the hands-free phone.

Please pick up.

After three torturous beeps, she came on the line. "Hello," she sounded unsure, hesitant.

He cringed. Did it mean she didn't want to talk to him? What should he say?

"Mommy, we all miss you! Daddy, I, and Chip love you! Please come back to us!" His daughter solved his dilemma.

Maybe this wasn't fair, but he didn't care. "I second that. We're on the way to Portland right now. We have something we need to do, and then we'd be thrilled to see you."

There was a pause as if she was fighting with herself. "I love you, too. All of you."

His initial wave of joy dissipated when Kristina added, "But I can't come back yet. Or see you. Not until I know... Never mind. I'm in Portland, too. I'm going to meet with Cullen in a few minutes."

His heart dropped. His fingers tightened around the steering wheel as he stared at the road ahead. Apparently, the way to Kristina was still a far and difficult journey. "So you returned to him."

"No. But I want you to know that whatever I'm doing is for your happiness." Her voice softened.

Well, hurting him by refusing to see him wasn't exactly making him happy. But he'd learned from his first marriage not to even try to understand women's logic.

A premonition entered his heart. Probably the consequences of the nightmare he'd seen the night before last.

He leaned forward and lowered his voice so his daughter wouldn't hear him. "One of the reasons I worry about Chelsea so much is... Who's going to raise her if something happens to me? Not to be vengeful, but I don't want her grandparents to do it."

"Nothing is going to happen to you. But if it makes you feel better, I'll do everything I can to take care of her if it does."

He felt a little lighter. "I know it's a lot to ask. And thank you. I miss you. I miss you with my entire being."

"We miss you!" Chelsea yelled from the backseat. Chip barked.

In other circumstances, he'd smile. "Oh, right. *We* miss you. I'm sure Chip is saying that, too."

"I miss you, too. All of you. So much." A sigh reverberated down the line. "Just be patient with me, okay?"

Staying away from Kristina wasn't easy, but as she disconnected, at least her words gave him hope.

The phone rang again. His heart fluttered. Maybe Kristina changed her mind.

The joy dimmed as he glanced on the dashboard. His lawyer.

He answered the call on the hands-free phone. "Hello, Mr. Cooper."

"Mr. Matthews, I have bad news. I wanted to let you know before our meeting, in case you'd like to find another lawyer." Official and stern, Cooper's voice cut into his thoughts.

Greg resisted the urge to grind his teeth. "I thought you were well qualified. The last time we spoke, you were sure you could get me full custody of Chelsea with only visitation rights for her grandparents."

"That's before I knew I'd be up against Cullen Langley."

Cullen? Seriously? How?

"The Ronfreys changed their lawyer. If you don't know what kind of reputation Langley has—"

"I know his reputation." More than just his reputation. "He's one of the top divorce lawyers in Portland." Suddenly, it all clicked into place.

Kristina didn't leave him because she didn't love him. Cullen blackmailed her. It might sound outlandish, but from what Greg surmised about the guy, it was more than probable. And she was meeting with him now to ensure Greg stayed with his little girl.

That's why she'd said whatever she did was for his happiness.

A mountain seemed to fall off his chest, and he could breathe more freely. "That's great news."

After a pause, Cooper came back on the line. "Excuse me? Did you hear what I said? I don't know if I can win the case now."

Cullen probably threatened Cooper. Or bribed him. Or both. "When did you know about that change?"

Another pause. "A few days ago."

Hmmm. But Cooper called only now. Greg decided to let it go. Looking for a new lawyer so late wouldn't be easy.

But with God's help, everything was possible.

And God had given him Kristina.

If he understood right, there was still hope for them.

"Let's discuss everything at the meeting. I want to see what you've done so far, and it'd better be a lot." Greg disconnected.

The deer leaped on the road right in front of his truck and froze. A quick glance in the mirrors told him a dark SUV was close behind, and a fourteen-wheeler was to his left.

Lord, please help us!

His blood going cold, he hit the brake. As Chelsea screamed in her booster seat and Chip barked, his thoughts were about his daughter.

CHAPTER FIFTEEN

KRISTINA FELT a sharp pain in her chest as she pulled up to the spacious building where her ex-husband had an office. Strange. Why would that be?

I guess I'm rattled after Greg's request to take care of Chelsea if something happens to him.

She loved the little girl, but to never see Greg again… She shuddered as she found a vacant spot and parked. She couldn't imagine her life without him. She just couldn't.

Or maybe she was nervous about seeing Cullen. Her gut twisted. But she was a different Kristina now, not the subdued, browbeaten wife he'd divorced.

She turned off the engine and marched inside the building.

Mimi, Cullen's secretary, rose from her chair when Kristina strode straight to Cullen's office door. "Ma'am, do you have an appointment?" Then her eyes widened. "Oh, Mrs. Langley..."

"Not anymore," Kristina said cheerfully and opened the door.

"Please, wait!" Mimi's scream didn't stop her.

Thankfully, Cullen was alone.

She strode to his gigantic desk.

A conceited smile curved his lips. "I knew you'd be back. Had no doubt, for that matter."

Drawing a deep breath for courage, she sat in the leather chair to be closer to his eye level. "Listen to me carefully because I'm not going to repeat myself. I'll never go back with you. And you'll never touch the lives of people I love with your dirty paws." Okay, she could've skipped the last two words.

He raised an eyebrow. "Really?"

"See, I'm not as dumb as you think. I overheard some of your conversations at home, and I remember every bit of it. You didn't always use honest tactics, did you?" She was bluffing, but he didn't need to know. It was more a feeling he'd done things behind his clients' backs than actual knowledge. Despite doubt inside, she kept her voice confident.

"You wouldn't dare to tell anyone." He waved a hand.

She wouldn't, and she hated to stoop to his methods.

Lord, please forgive me.

"Do you want to risk it?" She got up, walked around the table, and grabbed him by his expensive tie.

"You changed, Kristina. You changed a lot."

"True. You'll never walk over me again." She let the tie go, disgusted to touch him or his clothes. "You know, one of the scents in our house after I came back from visiting my brother... It took me a while to place it. But remember the celebration of your partner's birthday? The guy you're secretly afraid of, though you wouldn't admit it even to yourself? His wife wears the same perfume. What a coincidence, don't you think?"

"He won't believe you." Cullen's voice lacked confidence as he jumped to his feet.

"I found out you have a reputation of a skirt-chaser, so I wouldn't be so sure. Bottom line, if you ever try to put our daughters against me or come near the people I care about…" She paused for words. "I wouldn't advise it."

"Matthews will leave you soon enough. You'll see. He's just playing with you." His shoulders slumped forward as he slouched back into his chair. "We had over twenty years together. You can have it all back. The mansion, expensive cars, diamonds, everything. You can go to college, if you want, get that degree in interior design. I'll buy a restaurant for your mother. We'll travel overseas. Would you really throw it all away for a boy toy?"

She drew a sharp breath. "I wasn't the one who threw it all away. I'm grateful to you for giving me two wonderful daughters—I really am. But you nearly destroyed me with infidelities and emotional blackmail. God gave me a new life at forty when I least expected it. And Greg isn't a boy toy. He's the man I love. Leading a God-honoring life in my hometown, having a God-honoring family with him and Chelsea is all I want. Well, and Chip and Cupcake." She smiled.

Disappointment—or was it regret?—flashed in his cloudy-gray eyes, and he suddenly looked older. "Do you hate me?"

So much hope filled her there was no space for hatred. "No. I even wish you the best with your new girlfriend."

He curved further inward. "I don't have a girlfriend."

Huh. "What about all those women you had affairs with?"

He sighed. "They're boring, and they have no clue how to cook. I don't have anything to talk to them about. There's no warmth in them the way there was so much warmth in you. Their laughter is as fake as their eyelashes. And your laughter was always sincere, though I rarely made you laugh lately, did I?" He grabbed her hands. "I know you still love me. That's why you didn't tell our girls I was the one who filed for divorce or about how things were."

She eased her hands out of his. "I did it because I love *them*."

He shook his head as if still unable to believe her. "My offer won't stand for long. I can find plenty of women to be with."

"And if one of them loves you half as much as I once loved you or half as much as I love Greg, you'll be a very happy man." Peace inside her told her she meant it.

"So it's over between us?"

"Between us, it was over a long time ago. But it's a new beginning for me." She straightened her spine. "Thank you, Cullen, for giving me this chance to start fresh and find my true happiness."

The phone rang on his desk.

"Mrs. Ronfrey is on the line," Mimi chimed in. "She says she needs to speak to you urgently."

Kristina smiled sweetly. "Oh, one more thing. Mrs. Ronfrey withdrew the case after our pastor talked to her. Don't try to make her change her mind."

"Ask her to hold," Cullen told his secretary, then stepped to Kristina. "I'll do what you want. I won't try to change Mrs. Ronfrey's mind. But he'll leave you soon. He'll find someone younger and prettier and throw you out like garbage."

"Don't measure others with your own measure. Thankfully, there aren't many men like you." She turned to leave his office.

"And there are no other women like you." His whisper reached her as she opened the door.

Her heart sang as she strode to her car.

She sent Greg a quick text.

I'm coming back to Chapel Cove, and I'm not leaving again. I love you. Oh, how much I love you and Chelsea!

Just when she'd thought she'd been at the lowest point in her life, God had given her something amazing—love for a great man and a wonderful little girl and a talent she could hopefully realize.

Her heart shifted as her fingers tightened around the car door handle's cold surface. She still mourned her first marriage. Oh yes, she did. But now she could look forward to the future. Just like in childhood, when she and her friends ran toward the lighthouse on the cove, God gave her a new lighthouse to guide her.

She jumped into the car and smiled at her reflection in the rearview mirror. She'd learned to accept herself the way God created her and even the way she was aging.

No one ever made someone else happy by giving up their own dreams and their true self. Now God was helping her reach them.

After moving the key in the ignition, she turned on the radio and hummed along a Tejano song. She didn't need to worry any longer that, for some reason, Cullen couldn't stand Tejano music and she could never listen to it in his presence.

Grinning, she drove from the parking lot. She couldn't wait to tell Greg. He didn't answer her call on her hands-free phone, and she swallowed hard. She didn't know where in Portland he was, so she'd just have to see him when he returned to Chapel Cove.

But as she drove back to her hometown and kept calling him on her hands-free phone, her heart sank at long beeps and no answer. All her calls went to voicemail.

What was going on?

"Greg, please, please call me when you get this message. I… worry about you." She didn't care if she sounded desperate.

Their morning conversation rang in her ears. No, if he knew something was about to happen, he'd have told her.

A tow truck in the oncoming lane made her press on the brake. Two crumpled vehicles were on the side of the road. And one of them was...

No, it couldn't be!

No, no, no.

Her heart nearly stopped beating, and all the air in her car seemed to disappear as she struggled for her next breath. There were plenty of sapphire-colored trucks on the roads. It didn't mean this one was Greg's.

Tires squealed as she swerved to the side of the road. Without getting the key out of the ignition, leaving the door open, she sprinted to the blue truck.

As she saw the familiar license plate, her knees buckled. She almost sank to the ground.

Lord, please help them be okay. Please, please, please!

Terror claimed every cell in her body.

No. Think. Think. Think!

She rushed to the tow vehicle, which just parked, and jumped and waved to attract the driver's attention because she couldn't reach the handle.

While the driver seemed to be in no hurry to get out, she snatched her phone from her purse. Maybe she could find some news online. Or call somebody.

Finally, the guy in gray overalls and a matching cap wobbled outside.

"What happened here?" She didn't recognize her own voice—it was so loud. "Are the driver of the truck and the passenger okay?"

The man scratched his round chin. "Ma'am, I'm just towing the vehicles. I got no clue. I heard a deer ran in front of a truck." He spread his hands. "That's all I know."

She gasped, and her phone slid from her hands onto the asphalt. When she picked it up, it was useless. Her hands shook as she shoved the phone into her purse.

Okay, okay.

Doing her best to still her panic, she drew a deep breath filled with car fumes. Then she zoomed in on the guy. "May I borrow your phone?"

The man grimaced. "See, ma'am, I got a job to do here."

Her heart breaking, she grabbed his forearms. "Please. Please!"

His expression softened. "Somebody important to you was in there, huh?"

"Yes! The man and the child I love very much." She swallowed a hard lump in her throat.

"Whoa. Okay, but do it quick." He reached into his pocket and handed her his cell phone.

Her mind foggy, she tried to recall Nai's phone number but came up blank. She searched for Mr. and Mrs. Ronfrey's numbers on the internet but, in her haste, couldn't find them.

She'd just call Cullen's office. Kristina held her breath while listening to the beeps.

As soon as Mimi answered, Kristina said, "This is the former Mrs. Langley. I need to talk to Cullen. It's urgent."

"He's in a meeting." Mimi's officious tone said the no she didn't voice.

"I don't care. Tell him it's in his best interests to answer my call." She remembered all the times she'd called him, but he'd been too busy to talk to her. She'd always retreated then, feeling unimportant and unneeded.

Cullen came on the line. "What's so urgent?"

"I need Mrs. Ronfrey's phone number."

"She withdrew the suit." His voice was tired. "What else do you want?"

Kristina pursed her lips. "Listen, Cullen, I gave you twenty-two years of my life and two great kids. Give me that number. Now."

"Whoa. Hold on." Minutes later, he rattled off the phone number.

Her heart thundering, she disconnected and called Mrs. Ronfrey. Granted, they were not on the best terms, but she didn't have much choice.

Greg's former mother-in-law picked up on the second beep. After Kristina identified herself, the woman said, "Kristina, Greg and Chelsea were in an accident."

Then the line went dead.

Reluctant to believe her eyes, Kristina stared at the blank screen. "What happened?"

"Oh, my battery was low." The man's voice filtered through her mental fatigue.

"Do you have a charger in your vehicle?"

"Nope." He rolled on the balls of his feet. "I guess the guy you talked to wasn't the one you love?"

"No, it was my ex-husband." Going numb, she handed him the phone. "Thank you."

"Shaping up to be an interesting day." He walked to Greg's truck.

Her heart shattering in a million pieces, she cried all the way to Chapel Cove.

CHAPTER SIXTEEN

AFTER RIDING to Chapel Cove with the police, Greg rented a vehicle and had his daughter checked at Dr. Johnson's office. As much as Greg liked Dr. Johnson, this town really needed a pediatrician, and Greg had told him as much.

Then after getting a clean bill of health and calming down Mr. and Mrs. Ronfrey, Greg rescheduled his meeting with Cooper and buckled down his little girl.

"So sorry you had to go through this, honey." He placed a kiss atop her head, breathing in the sweet scent of her mango shampoo.

Cold traveled down his back. That was one close encounter.

"It's okay, Daddy. I prayed to God, and God saved us." She blinked her baby blues.

Oh, the amazing strength of his child's faith!

Time for him to start praying and talking to God, have a real heartfelt conversation like he used to have when Sally was alive. And where better than in God's house?

He adjusted his girl's ponytail, which slid down a little. "I want to go to church for a few minutes. I want to talk to God. Is it okay with you?"

"Yes, Daddy. Grandpa told me that my mommy always said, 'What could be more important than talking to God?' So I talked to the Lord."

His throat constricted as he jumped into the driver's seat. He'd never forget Sally, but he'd finally learned to live without her. "Did... God reply to you?"

"Yes. He said that one day I'll have a new mommy, and she'll love me very much."

As Greg turned the keys in the ignition, something prickled behind his eyes—good tears, the ones that could cleanse your soul. "Kristina does love you very much."

His heart swelled as he drove carefully from the clinic's parking lot. That simple text from Kristina that she was coming back and she loved him... It made his heart dance with happiness. He couldn't answer her calls while he'd talked to the police, but while he'd waited for Chelsea to be seen in the clinic, Kristina had been the one who hadn't answered his calls.

Worry tightened his gut. No, probably her phone battery died or something.

Minutes later, he and Chelsea entered the church.

Holding her tiny hand, he slipped into a pew. Then he helped her climb on the upholstered seat and knelt.

As he lifted his eyes to a high ceiling, serenity entered his heart.

Dear Heavenly Father, thank You for saving our lives today. I'm sorry if I doubted Your love for us. Going on without Sally was just so difficult. I know I missed Sunday services and wallowed in my misery. I wasn't a good servant to You. But You brought me near to You again. Your love is limitless, and Your mercy is limitless, too. Thank You.

Greg stayed still with the Lord.

Chelsea whispered something as if she had her own conversation with the Lord.

He lifted his eyes again.

Did You mean Kristina for me and as Chelsea's new mother? Is she the one?

For some time, he didn't receive any answer.

And then he could hear the organ playing, as if in a dream. As he looked around, he could imagine the pews decorated with bows the color of sunrise, something between marmalade and honey. It was like a dream he could see awake. In a pretty marmalade-colored silk dress, Chelsea ran forward, spreading rose petals around herself. Nai and then Reese in gorgeous gowns of the same color were walking down the aisle. Twin girls, their facial features resembling Kristina's, dressed in the same hue silk gowns followed them.

And then…

Smiling Kristina in a breathtaking wedding dress was moving slowly, accompanied by an older man and a woman.

The image disappeared, but he stared into space for some time, his heart beating fast. This was his imagination, of course, but he saw it so clearly….

Kristina was the answer to his prayers. Even those he'd never said.

We love You, Lord. Thank You.

After Greg and his daughter left the church, he placed her into the booster seat. With a deep longing inside him, he wanted so badly to see Kristina, but he needed to consider Chelsea's wishes. "Where to now? Are you hungry?"

His daughter glanced at the puppy, who yipped. "Let's go see my new mommy. Chip says so, too."

He hid a smile as he closed the car door, then slipped into the driver's seat. He glanced back. "He says that, huh?"

"Yep." Chelsea's ponytail bounced as she nodded her confidence.

Soon Greg pulled up to Kristina's rental and stifled disappointment. Her car wasn't in the driveway. She must still be with Cullen. He didn't let jealousy distract him.

Thankfully, his daughter and he were fine after nearly hitting a deer. His truck had to be towed due to the car behind them ramming it, but neither one of them even had a scratch.

Thank You, Lord, for saving Chelsea and me.

As he glanced back at his treasure, he knew God truly loved him, even when Greg doubted His love. Just like six years ago God had sent an amazing woman to draw Greg near Him, He now sent another amazing woman to do the same.

"Well, sweetheart…"

"Mommy will be back soon." As the puppy barked, his child continued, "Chip thinks so, too."

A growl of a motor and an appearance of an old sedan proved her right.

"Yay! She's back!" Chelsea clapped.

His heart overflowed with love for two precious girls as he stepped out of his rental.

Kristina's sedan stopped abruptly near the curb. The door opened, and she fell rather than climbed out of her car. Her dark eyes went wide, and she opened her mouth, then closed it. Tears streaked her face, leaving black mascara rivers.

Unease replaced his joy. Was she okay? Maybe she felt sick. His rib cage constricted as he rushed to her.

She slid down, and he barely caught her before she hit the ground.

Worry slammed into him full force. "Kristina! Are you unwell? What's happening? Do I need to call 911?"

Droplets sparkled on her eyelashes. "I'm fine. I–I saw your truck. I thought…"

"Oh, darling." His heart expanding, he hugged her. "We're fine. Chelsea is fine. I'm fine. The driver behind me is fine. Chip is fine. Even the deer I barely avoided hitting is fine. I saw him walk away."

"Praise God!" she whispered against his chest.

He said his own prayer of gratitude.

"I was so scared… I don't know how to live without you and Chelsea." She sniffled.

Chip barked from the truck.

She moved back and smiled. "And Chip. Oh, and I have good news. The Ronfreys are not going to try to get custody. Our pastor had a conversation with them."

"Praise God. They called me and told me already." Humble as always, Kristina obviously hadn't taken credit for talking them out of it, too, by explaining she'd never stop them from seeing Chelsea. "And I want to thank you for talking to them." He stared into her beautiful brown eyes.

The image he'd had in the church reappeared. He knew what was in his heart.

It might not be the right time or the place, and he didn't even have a ring. He hesitated. Kristina deserved the most romantic proposal ever and a large diamond ring. But he didn't want to wait, and surely, she'd understand?

He dropped on one knee. "I shouldn't be rushing things. But I decided to be selfish right now. I love you. I love everything about you. Your shy smile. Your kind eyes. Your willingness to work hard for your dream. Your dedication to the people you love. I love every tiny dot in your brown eyes and the way your hair moves in the wind. I can't wait to spend the rest of my life with you, and I want it to start as soon as possible. I know I'm speaking for both Chelsea and myself when I ask you to make me the happiest man alive. Marry me."

She gasped, and her palm flew to her mouth. For a few torturous moments, she stared at him. Then she jumped up and down like a kid. "Yes. Yes. Yes!"

Exhilaration filled him.

He lifted her and whirled around.

He wanted to hold her forever, but somebody else was anxious to see her. As well as get out of the booster seat.

He wrapped his arm around Kristina's shoulder, and they approached his rental SUV.

Just a few days ago, he hadn't thought he could be this happy.

Thank You, Lord, for all this.

After he removed his daughter from the seat, she stretched her arms toward Kristina. "Mommy, you won't leave us anymore?"

Kristina's eyes sparkled again, but he hoped this time they were happy tears. "No, sweetie. There's no other place I'd rather be than with you and your father."

Chip barked from the truck.

Kristina chuckled. "And Chip and Cupcake."

"Ditto." He placed a kiss on her mascara-streaked cheek.

"And I can have Taco back?" His little girl grinned.

Kristina smiled as she leaned into him. "Yes, of course, you can have Taco back."

Chelsea sighed contentment. "Love you, Mommy, Daddy."

God could often give unexpected gifts, even in the midst of suffering and turmoil. And as Greg wrapped his arms around his bride-to-be and his daughter, he held such precious gifts in his arms.

EPILOGUE

Three months later…

STANDING IN the church dressing room, Kristina whirled in front of the large oval mirror.

Nai picked up the bridal bouquet with fragrant peach-colored roses. "Yes, you're the most beautiful bride in the world. You're simply glowing."

"That's because she's happy." Reese spread the veil over Kristina's shoulders. "You're happy, right?"

Kristina's heart fluttered. "Are you kidding? I'm absolutely, deliriously happy. Hmmm. All three of us brides at forty. Who'd think?" Then she brightened. "Greg told me one of his aunts is engaged at seventy, so I'm a very young and, of course, absolutely gorgeous bride."

"Of course." Nai smiled.

Kristina hugged her best friends. "And just look at both of you. You're knockouts in bridesmaids' dresses."

She stepped aside so the girls could see themselves in the mirror.

"Reese is. There's a reason she was a supermodel." Nai grimaced. "I don't know if marmalade suits me much. But you always liked that 'color of sunset'."

"Nai, you're beautiful just the way God created you. And you know it." Kristina wiggled her finger at her friend.

Then her heartbeat skyrocketed. In just a few minutes, she'd marry Greg, the man she loved with her whole heart, and she was gaining a wonderful daughter. Kristina couldn't help herself. She opened the door ajar, peeped in the slit, and felt the corners of her lips lift. Chelsea was going to be the most adorable flower girl ever. Thankfully, they'd managed to talk her out of sharing that role with Chip.

And Kristina's parents were talking again and even agreed to give her away together. Her father had traveled from Paraguay for the occasion. Kristina, Roman, and Greg had offered to help her mother open a restaurant, but she'd decided against it. She'd rather stay retired, especially considering her son and daughter had started giving her monthly checks again.

Kristina's gaze traveled over the pews, decorated with flowers and bows matching her bridesmaids' dresses. Greg's parents had flown from England and met her in Chapel Cove three days ago. According to Greg, they had adored her, because, really, "how could anyone not?"

"Did you see him?" Reese's voice was strained. Strange.

Kristina closed the door. "Greg? No. Not yet." Her heart fluttered. "But in a few minutes…"

"Oh. I meant Cullen." Reese looked down as if sensing she'd said too much. "I spotted him enter the church earlier. Alone. He seemed subdued."

Nai snorted. "As he should. To lose such treasure as our Kristina."

Kristina leaned against the door. "Divorce is difficult. And heart-wrenching. And it leaves you empty for a long time. But I made peace with it. God can turn the biggest disasters in our lives into the best opportunities if we open ourselves to the possibilities. I'm glad to be in Chapel Cove again and close to you, Mom, Roman. Not to mention to find a new family with Greg and Chelsea and their pets."

"Yeah. Such a tiny detail. We're happy to be together again, too." Nai grinned as she spread the train carefully around Kristina. "And your hands-on interior decorating business is doing great."

Kristina's fluttering heart expanded. "Partly thanks to your and Greg's referrals. I'm taking college courses online to improve my skills. I'm happy Greg's sports equipment store is pretty busy, too, especially during windsurfing season."

"You fulfilled the part on your list where you wanted to do something crazy," Reese added. "You went snowboarding with Greg in Colorado. Did it take him a long time to talk you into it?"

"Took me a while to talk *him* into it. And I was pretty scared. But it was an exhilarating experience, and I loved seeing happiness in his eyes. He's a fantastic snowboarder. And no, I'm not being partial. He has tons of comments to his snowboarding videos." Joy filled Kristina's whole being. "Hmmm, I did click off many items on my bucket list, not exactly by the age of forty, but close enough."

"You certainly did." A photo-ready grin tweaked Reese's lips. "Maybe it's time for us to make lists of things to do before we're eighty."

"Not a bad idea. All in all, I finally found myself. And I found Greg and Chelsea. And Chip and Cupcake."

Even Greg's former in-laws had changed a lot and now treated her nearly with the kindness she treated them. They even agreed to pet-sit Chip and Cupcake when Greg, Kristina, and Chelsea went on a honeymoon to India. Not only because it was one of the items on Kristina's bucket list. Chelsea needed to see real elephants.

Reese's eyes went misty. "You'll make me cry. You've got everything. What else can you wish for?"

Kristina hesitated. Should she tell them? Well, of course! She leaned to her friends. "You'll probably think I'm crazy. I already have three great daughters. And, um, I'm forty. But I'd be thrilled to have a little boy with Greg who'd be just like him. I want to pray for it. And if it's God's will…"

Nai lifted her chin. "I don't think that's crazy at all."

Reese quirked an eyebrow. "Kristina, not that I think it's a bad idea. But be careful what you wish for. You've already had one set of twins. You might be chasing two boys soon."

Kristina laughed again. "I'd love that. And I know Greg. He'll help me every step of the way. He's a talented snowboarder and a great businessman. But he said that since Chelsea was born the most important job he'd ever wanted to do was to be a father."

The door burst open, and Leanna and Reanna rushed inside. "So sorry we're late."

Kristina hugged her darling daughters, already dressed in bridesmaids' dresses. They did grow up so fast. "No, you're right in time. And you look… wow."

"Mom, it's you who looks wow." Leanna leaned to her and whispered, "Sorry I treated you badly after your divorce." Then she eased back. "We love you very much."

"Ditto." Reanna threw a quick glance at herself in the mirror. She was always more self-conscious of the two. Then she turned back to her mother. "And it's cool to have such a young stepdad and a new sister."

Nai stepped forward. "As much as I enjoy this family gathering, it's time. Let's get you married off, amiga."

Minutes later, Kristina walked down the aisle toward the man she loved so much.

Greg's eyes shone brightly as he stood near his best men, Roman and Greg's friends from Portland. After her soon-to-be husband had met the real Roman, they'd fast become friends.

More handsome than ever in his tuxedo, Greg smiled at her.

Her heart was overflowing with happiness.

She lifted her eyes up to heaven and thanked God for all His wonderful gifts.

THE END

Thank you for reading *Love Me*. If you write even several words on Amazon, BookBub, and/or Goodreads, it'll mean a lot to me. You can make a difference! I'm grateful to every person who reads my books, and every review matters to me. Authors depend so much on reviews and recommendations, and it's a great joy for us when our books find new homes.

It's not easy to start over at forty, and often sad things that happened to us pull us down. *Love Me* is close to my heart, and not only because my age is near the heroine's and I found myself making difficult choices much later in life than I wanted.

There are so many romances written about love in people's twenties and thirties, but what about the rest of us? I was eager to write a story where I could easily relate to the heroine in many aspects, including the age, and about a good, honest man capable of great love for her. And so I did. And I'll be honest, little Chelsea stole my heart!

I hope you enjoyed Greg's and Kristina's story. If you didn't have a chance to read Book 1 in the Chapel Cove Romances series, I hope you'll check out Reese's story in *Remember Me* by Marion Ueckermann. And please be on the lookout for Nai's story in Book 3 in the series, *Cherish Me* by Autumn Macarthur. I know I'm partial, but I loved Nai and Mateo's story! And then, Roman's and (maybe) Aileen's story is waiting to be written. If you'd like to know when new books in this series are released, please follow the Chapel Cove Romances page on Amazon:
https://www.amazon.com/Chapel-Cove-Romances/e/B07PZKWZMR
We had so much fun working on this series and will be happy if you enjoy these books.

I do love hearing from readers, and if you email me at alexaverde7@gmail.com or visit me on my social media links mentioned on my author page you'll make my heart sing. And if you'd like to know about my upcoming releases, please follow me on Amazon. Of course, I'd be thrilled if you looked at my other books, and I pray and hope they'll bring you joy and encouragement.

For giveaways, news, free ebooks, and recipes, please sign up for my newsletter: http://www.alexaverde.com/contact.html#newsletter. Subscribers have access to exclusive subscriber-only contests, subscriber free ebooks, and book news (while they are subscribed). Emails won't arrive more than weekly, your email address will never be passed on to anyone else, and you can unsubscribe at any time. Also, you'll get the download link for a FREE sweet Christian romance ebook, *Season of Mercy*, as soon as you confirm your email address as a thank-you gift.

Thank you very much for sharing your time with me and my books, and I hope we'll meet again. God bless you.

With love,

Alexa Verde

ACKNOWLEDGMENTS

Many thanks to God for helping me write this book and sending two amazing authors to work with, Autumn Macarthur and Marion Ueckermann.

I also want to thank my wonderful readers who helped in different ways to make *Love Me* what it is now: Kathy and Rose for suggesting a name for the kitten (Cupcake), to Jenn, Bobby, and Natalya for suggesting Chip or Chocolate Chip as the name of the pet, and to Jenn for helping me choose the breed. Heartfelt thanks to Debbie, Paula, Marylin, Sue, and Linda for beta reading this book!

ABOUT ALEXA VERDE

ALEXA VERDE writes sweet, wholesome books about faith, love, and murder. She has had 200 short stories, articles, and poems published in the five languages that she speaks. She has bachelor's degrees in English and Spanish, a master's in Russian, and enjoys writing about characters with diverse cultures. She's worn the hats of reporter, teacher, translator, model (even one day counts!), caretaker, and secretary, but thinks that the writer's hat suits her the best.

After traveling the world and living in both hemispheres, she calls a small town in south Texas home. The latter is an inspiration for the fictional setting of her series *Rios Azules Christmas* and *Secrets of Rios Azules*. Please visit her online, on Facebook and Twitter.

Please visit Alexa's website for more of her books:
http://www.alexaverde.com/

You can also find Alexa on social media:
Facebook : alexaverdeauthor
Twitter : AlexaVerde3
Goodreads : 8180452.Alexa_Verde
Bookbub : authors/alexa-verde
Amazon : Alexa-Verde/e/B00KCA754C

TITLES BY ALEXA VERDE

Christian Contemporary Romance

CHAPEL COVE ROMANCES
Love Me *(Book 2)*
Other books in this tri-author series are by:
Marion Ueckermann and Autumn Macarthur

THE POTTER'S HOUSE
Heart Unbroken *(Book 1)*
Heart Healed *(Book 2)*
Heart Restored *(Book 3)*

RIOS AZULES CHRISTMAS SERIES
In Love by Christmas Box Set (Season of Miracles,
Season of Joy, Season of Hope)
Season of Miracles *(Book 1)* (Arturo and Lana)
Season of Joy *(Book 2)* (Dylan and Joy)
Season of Hope *(Book 3)* (Brandon and Kelly)

RIOS AZULES ROMANCES: THE MACALISTERS SERIES
Season of Romance *(Book 1)* (Andrey and Melinda)
Season of Love *(Book 2)* (Petr and Lacy-Jane)
Season of Amor *(Book 3)* (Ray and Sylvia)

Season of Mercy